The Leap

Jonathan Stroud

Northern Plains Public Library
Ault Colorado

MIRAMAX BOOKS
HYPERION PAPERBACKS FOR CHILDREN
NEW YORK

If you purchased this book without a cover, you should be aware that this book is stolen property. It was reported as "unsold and destroyed" to the publisher, and neither the author nor the publisher has received any payment for this "stripped" book.

Text copyright © 2001 by Jonathan Stroud
All rights reserved. No part of this book may be reproduced or transmitted in any form or by any means, electronic or mechanical, including photocopying, recording, or by any information storage and retrieval system, without written permission from the publisher. For information address Hyperion Books for Children, 114 Fifth Avenue, New York, New York 10011-5690.

Originally published in the United Kingdom by Random House Children's Books. Reprinted by permission.

First United States edition
First Hyperion Paperback edition, 2004
1 3 5 7 9 10 8 6 4 2

Printed in the United States of America
This book is set in 11-point Adobe Garamond.

Library of Congress Cataloging-in-Publication Data on file.
ISBN 0-7868-5195-3

Visit www.hyperionbooksforchildren.com

For Nana and to the memory

of K. A. Stroud

One

In the green water, among the rushing bubbles, he is looking at me still. His face shows white against the moss and the weed fronds.

As I watch, he mouths my name through the soundless water. An explosion of bubbles erupts from his lips. They race forward and cling to my eyes and face and for a moment I am blind. Then they boil upward toward the daylight and I can see again. And I just have time to catch his eyes once more, as they turn away from me into the dark, and his face is swallowed by the greenness all around.

He is gone. I open my eyes. The ward is dark, and someone is crying. I know him without turning: it is the boy in the end bed, nearest the orange night-light. Small and hollow-cheeked, with his leg in plaster, he has often cried before. Tonight he is lonely, sick, and homesick, and it is many hours before his mother will visit him again. His weeping sounds thin in the shrouded ward. I wait, watching out of the corner of my eye. Soon the crisp, efficient shadow of the nurse appears beside his bed. The outline of her hand reaches down and touches his hidden face. A murmured question comes, soft and comforting, then the small sounds of his gulped replies. He sinks down into the high pillows. She straightens and melts away. I lie back and close my eyes.

Max does not come again. Try as I might, I see nothing—instead I become aware of the starched restriction of the bedclothes, pressing close against my body. My arms are pinioned by my sides, and only my head, in its deep halo of pillows, is free to turn. I have been tucked in well. To secure me any tighter, they would have had to use a straitjacket.

My legs fidget under the taut, clean sheets. It is my sixth night here, and tomorrow, perhaps, they'll let me go home. Even if they do, I'll have to see a doctor every week—and not a lung doctor either. My chest *did* give me trouble, but it's been fine for days now and still they've kept me in, using it as a pretext to watch me, talk with me, and prove I'm mad.

A single car is moving in the night, far below the window. Around it, the city sleeps. I lie awake, thinking of Max and what has become of him.

They are careful now never to mention his name. But he is there all right, heavy in their faces—in Mum's and the doctors'—and in the eyes of the nice policewoman who did her best to make me give my story up. They seem unable to invoke him, scared of what he might do. And I never help them out, not even when their meaningful pauses invite me to talk about Max again. They hold the door open, but I never walk through. I learn fast, you see. After the first time, and after Mum, I'm saying nothing. I've said nothing for so long now that I think they wonder if I am blanking him out. And I *know* that is what Mum is hoping.

Fine, let them think it. Let them leave me alone, to lie here and think of Max.

I like the darkness. It is both a veil and a screen for memories to be hung upon. To the nurse, the homesick boy, the others sleeping hammocked in the heavy black warmth of the ward, there is nothing to be seen. But for me, the room is brightly lit with images crowding down on every side. I can view them all, alone.

I rerun a scene. Max and I, on our bikes. Away from his street and down the hill road, out of town. Past the canal, the pubs, the blank fronts of the factory buildings, with Max always in front, me always behind. Under the overpass and the last estate and out into the September fields, with the sun shining and our legs going and the wind squeezing tears out of our eyes. A good run, good enough for sweat to break out on my back, and my thigh muscles to start complaining.

Through the brown fields, slower now. Max began to tire, and I made up the gap, coming alongside him. He was red in the face, grinning with concentration. We came to the little bridge over the river. There were willows by the water and an unkempt meadow that didn't look too soft or wet. I was for trying it, since the water was deep enough for fish, but Max said no, he knew a better place. We cycled on.

Somewhere in the ward the night nurse's buzzer goes. I hear it faintly, a muffled sound. On padded feet she comes, prowling down the corridor, looking for the flashing light. In my bay, everyone is sleeping—except for me, and I am very still. She passes and her footfalls fade. For some reason a desperate weight grips my stomach and I feel the prickle of tears coming. Stop being stupid, Charlie—think back, play the images on the night screen. Watch and remember.

I had been to the mill before. Mum had taken me there, with James, last summer. Overgrown with weeds and thorn, the little path meandered along between two ugly electric fences. We wheeled our bikes up, breathing fast, to join the dirt road that ran over the cattle grid to the millstream. A public right-of-way the track was, though the mill itself, behind its high wall, was private and operational, supplying some little baking firm uptown.

Men's voices sounded over the redbrick wall. The millstream disappeared into a low-slung arch in the stonework. We went around the side, past the mill to the back of the buildings and the wheel.

It was turning. We stood at a vantage point on the lip of the brick, looking down at the hellish cauldron of foam and churning milk. The wall was drenched in spray and the bricks were covered in sponge-wet moss. The wheel roared in the shades below the parapet, huge wooden cusps erupting from the stream, rising out and upward in an endless arc, then ducking away again, leaving us deafened. The air was wet and cold and cooled us quickly after our ride. Max clambered out onto the rough stone lip above the frothing water, hanging his legs out over the edge to embrace the light white spray.

The image goes out. I realize I am staring into space like a sightless fish, and all the muscles in my neck are hurting. I wrestle myself into a new position, fighting the sheets to get on to my side. It ruins the nice matron's tucking, but I haven't moved properly since visitors' hour, when Mum and James finally left. It was James's first time. He was sheepish about the whole thing and only caught my eye once when Mum was telling one of her nonstories. But he was upset too. You could tell because he kissed me when he left, in an awkward sort of way. I wonder how much he's heard, and what he thinks of me. The pillows bite into the side of my face, and my cheek feels raw and rough. I want to rub it, but I stay quite still now, looking toward the window and the night, where the wheel is turning.

Below the mill wheel was a sluice, and beyond that the stream continued along until it opened out into a shady mill pool, fringed with stone. This was where Max intended us to fish.

"I saw some big ones here once." He flung his bike down at the foot of a plum tree and took his fishing rod from the pack strapped to its back. There was a ring of plum trees around the pool, each one hunched and shriveled with age. I considered them while Max fixed the bait. The plums in the branches hanging out over the water were ripe and dark.

Max was ready. We sat down on the stone lip of the quiet pool and he made his first cast. The water was still and idle-looking, and the sun reflected lazily off the surface. It was a hot afternoon.

Thrushes sang from the trees and the sun beat down on our backs and we caught nothing. Every now and then, big fat carp with white eyes and ghostly swathes of gray on their sides rose up slowly from the murk and hovered just below our dangling bait, for all the world as if they were watching. Not once did they try to bite, but just stared dumbly, before turning away with a swift flick of the tail. Max was very bad at fishing. I said so. He threw his rod to one side and we lay back gazing at the sky.

Lying in the bed, a dull pain flashes in my calf, though the bandage is long gone and the marks are fading. The doctors say that Max must have scratched my leg and I hate them for that more than anything else. Not because they don't believe me—they don't believe anything I've told them. No, what makes me mad is that they think I kicked out for the surface while he was alive and reaching up for me. *Kicked out and left him.* And they don't tell me I'm a coward to my face, but just ask me how I am, and look regretful, and refuse to mention Max by name.

And anyone could tell you he didn't have long nails to scratch with.

He was probably biting them then, lying by the pool with the midafternoon sun warming his face. He hates being still, gets restless. I was dozing beside him, as the heat and the long ride began to catch up with me. But I wasn't allowed to lie quiet for long. After a minute or so, he stirred and spoke.

"Well, if fishing's out, let's swim instead."

I raised myself sluggishly and looked at the water. "Don't be stupid," I said. "It's not that hot, and I haven't brought my costume."

Max laughed from below. He was lying back with his arm shielding his eyes from the sun. "Nor have I," he said. "I'll dive starkers. I don't care."

I shrugged. "*You* may not. *I* need a costume."

"You're just chicken. I wouldn't look." Max leaned up on his elbows and surveyed the pool. I said nothing. I wasn't going in and I didn't think Max was either. His enthusiasm seemed to have dampened down a bit. Maybe it was the quiet stillness of the pool and maybe it wasn't.

"Off you go, then," I said, helpfully. "I'll guard your clothes."

Max grunted. "In a bit." He looked around him restlessly. Something had put him out of sorts.

"We should have brought lunch with us," he said. "There's no shop for miles."

I raised a lazy finger. "Plenty of free food around. Hop up if you're hungry."

The plum tree's heavy-laden branches hung out over the mill pool, warped by years of gales. Max eyed them narrowly. A new challenge was revealed.

"Maybe I will, if you're chicken."

"Throw some down for me." I lay back and closed my eyes. There was a bit of scuffling and a couple of curses, and when I risked a look I saw Max's feet and bottom rapidly disappearing into the tree above.

"Watch it, Max. You'll be over the water."

"He who dares gets the plums."

He inched out along a sturdy branch until he sat about two feet beyond the stone lip of the mill pool. There he wedged himself into position, plucked a purple-black plum from a nearby clump and shoved it whole into his mouth. In a matter of seconds he had devoured it. He spat the stone into the water where it disappeared with a dull *splot*. I called for my share, but I had to wait until he'd dispatched another two before he threw me one. It was very ripe and very sweet.

I sat on the ground between the tree and the edge and ate a couple more. Quite soon I lost my appetite. Whether or not it was the fruit, I had a dull ache in my stomach and could only wonder that Max kept popping plums into his mouth, undaunted by sheer quantity. The fall of plum stones continued like a light rain.

Then the rain stopped. Max must finally be stuffed. I looked up at him. He was very still on his perch, with his head tilted on one side. Surely he couldn't have fallen asleep? No, his eyes were wide open, and so was his mouth, and he was gazing down into the water six feet or so below him. His hands were white and gripped the branch as if he feared to fall. I followed his gaze to the pool, but saw only the reflection of the sunlight, which hurt my eyes.

"What's up, Max?" I called out sharply; Max seldom stopped to look at anything. "Hey, Max, pass us another."

There was no answer. I called again. Still he gazed down into the dreamy depths of the pool and made no move or sound. A pang of panic gripped my chest, though Max had often ignored me in the past, just as I had often ignored him.

"Max! Say something! Snap out of it—if this is a joke, it's not funny. You look like a fool with your mouth open like that. Get a grip." I didn't know why I was so concerned, and that irritated me in itself. "Come on, answer me—"

I broke off. Suddenly, as if responding to a call, Max swung his legs so that they were hanging off the branch and he was sitting looking down between them. And then, with barely a pause, and with no break in his concentrated gaze, he gave a violent push forward and toppled into space.

He fell without a sound, and the waters of the mill pool closed over him. I sprang to my feet with a cry and leaned out over the edge, scanning the surface. No bubbles rose. There was one swirl of a wave, just one, and then the surface was still again, as calm as ever.

I waited.

Time froze at the edge of the pool. I waited, waited for his head to reappear.

Here in the quiet night the boy in the end bed has woken and is crying again. This time the nurse does not hear him. He cries on, his weeping draining away into the darkness. My eyes are wide open, staring. The image on the night screen is frozen; the surface is still. Slowly, slowly, he cries himself to quietness. Silence fills the ward.

A wood pigeon called—its sleepy sound cuts me like a knife. And with that, the birdsong that had broken off at the single splash suddenly resumed. Time started up once more and I kicked off my shoes and dived into the pool.

As I hit the water, the warm sun was peeled off my back as if I had been flayed. My body stung with the cold, my ears rang with silence. All the little flitterings and soothing cries of that late summer day were left behind. I opened my eyes and saw around me a green-gray void. Behind me were the stones of the mill pool's edge, caked in long green fronds that stroked my legs with clammy tips.

I passed them by. Around and below was an emerald green emptiness, speared here and there by weak shafts of sunlight that had broken through the surface and now faded away into the depths. The pool was very deep.

Far off, in the green reaches, I saw Max. He was swimming, but swimming down, his face turned from the hot sun. I pursued him with a knot of panic in my belly and the blood pounding in my head, but hard as I beat my legs, I could not catch him. And then I noticed other things moving in the water; pale thin women with long hair streaming like river moss, who wrapped their arms around him as he spun in the waters of the mill pool.

I swam toward them, and they turned, and Max's face was white and his eyes were open, but I knew he couldn't see me anymore. He smiled and the women smiled with him, and they could see me all right—they were looking at me with eyes as green as buried pebbles.

One of them kicked her legs and floated over to me, reaching out with long thin fingers and smiling. Her touch was cold, like a mountain brook in winter, and when she opened her mouth, I heard bubbling like water between deep stones. Her hair drifted languidly before my eyes, her fingers brushed my neck, and I felt a laziness grow over me, a sleepy desire to float amid the quiet things in this peaceful pool, to drift among the rocks and broken wood and lost, forgotten things and never feel the harshness of the sun again. But I had seen the eyes of my friend Max, and seen his skin, all pasty-white like feet dangled in a river through a summer's afternoon. And suddenly I longed for the touch of wind, the endless colors of the sky and earth and for the sounds that fade in layers across the hills.

So I set about her with my fists, and tore myself from her slender arms. Her mouth opened in startled rage and the water around us turned to foam. I kicked upward toward the dim daylight arches as her fury sent a million bubbles rushing around me.

Then a hand reached up out of the foam and grabbed my ankle. In my terror, I lashed downward with my free foot and made sharp contact with something solid. The hand released me, but dragged its nails across my leg as it fell away.

Now the bubbles seemed to carry me upward in a cushion of spume, and the light grew in brightness till it burst upon my head with all the heat of the late summer air. I floated in the very center of the mill pool, with the blood throbbing in my wounded calf. The bubbles vanished and the thrushes sang in the plum trees. The afternoon was two minutes older than when my feet had left the edge, but that moment had receded in my head to distant depths and the birdsong sounded strange. I swam to the edge and hauled myself out onto the hot stone, from where I gazed stupidly at the calm waters of the mill pool, which hid my friend forever. My lungs breathed air, but cold green water filled my heart.

Two

After an hour I began to expect Mum back. An hour was long enough for a visit, especially when you've left your son in the car without food or drink. You could probably get into trouble for that, like leaving your dog in the backseat without opening the window.

Time dragged. I'd learned my lesson from the last time and had brought along a book, but like a fool it was one I'd nearly finished, and after fifteen minutes it was done and dusted and I was just as bored as ever. I read the cover blurb and counted the number of lies the publishers had printed about the excellence of the writing. This took another minute. Then I had to fall back on my own initiative, which sadly meant watching the comings and goings in the hospital car park. I tried to add a bit of spice to it by guessing the ailment of each passerby, but that didn't help much. They were either too easy, like the man with the broken leg who swore at the woman who was wheeling him in (I hoped she'd push him down the slope into the bins at the back of the hospital cafeteria, but she didn't), or too difficult like most of the rest. They were all just pale and drawn looking, and often I couldn't tell if they were patients themselves or just visiting. One way or another, it was depressing viewing.

Ten more minutes trudged by. I tried telling myself I was angry with Mum for bringing me along at all, and that I would rather have been back home watching TV. But it didn't wash. Really, I was furious about being kept in the car like some little kid, when I should have been in there, doing the elder-brother bit, looking after Charlie.

I'd seen her the day before for the first time. But I blew it; Mum did all the talking and I just sat there like a lemon saying nothing. What was stupid was that I had plenty to say, or thought I had. It had been a whole week, and I hadn't set eyes on her since the night before it happened, when we played snooker together in the spare room. Charlie won 3–2, on the pink in the last. I'd tried to extend the series to best of seven, but Mum had yelled at us through the wall and we'd gone to bed. When I got up, she'd already gone around to Max's place.

For some reason, the thought of that snooker game made me feel a bit weepy. I tried to find a tissue in the car, but there was only an oily one under the seat, so I used my sleeve instead. A fat lady chose that moment to try and squeeze her bulk down between our car and the next one. She caught my eye just when my nose was in mid-sleeve. I felt embarrassed, not because of my sleeve, but because my eyes were still watery. It gave me intense satisfaction to watch her struggling on between the cars, and even more when she had to open her driver's door and pour herself, wheezing and panting, through the tiny aperture onto her seat. Then I remembered she was probably back from visiting a dying husband or something, and that made me feel guilty and even worse than before.

I thought of Mum going in, wearing the same pinched, weary look that all the other people I'd seen had had, and wished once again she'd taken me in for moral support. But Mum likes to keep things as simple as possible and having me around somehow complicated matters. I think she wanted to keep me separate from Charlie for as long as possible, until she was sure Charlie was all right again. I'd only got in the day before because I'd started a shouting match in the hospital reception.

Charlie had seemed calm enough when we'd sat down, and had talked reasonably with us about unimportant things. There wasn't any wild light in her eyes; she was looking forward to getting out, she said, and was bored in there. Mum gave her some books. She looked fine, just a bit pale—but there was something odd about her that I couldn't put my finger on. Perhaps it was how quiet she was. Normally, she and Mum can't go five minutes without an argument starting, and even then, when she was being extra careful, Mum came up with a few beauties that should have roused Charls into action. But she just sat there, pale and composed, ignoring the cues. I was silent too, thinking about what Mum had told me on that first dreadful morning, when she'd come back hollow-eyed from her vigil at the bedside. About the accident. About what they found in the pool. But most of all, about Charlie's story.

When Mum had wept it out, it had made no sense to me. I couldn't connect with it, I couldn't link it to my sister at all. For the whole week it had festered in my mind and I was no nearer to digesting it. And then, when I saw her sitting up in bed, quiet, polite, and completely bored, the whole thing hit me all over again—I mean the utter impossibility of what she'd said—and I found I was too upset to talk.

A figure was walking swiftly through the car park. I was looking right at it, but it took a few moments before I realized it was Mum.

I leaned over and opened the driver's door from the inside. Mum flopped down on the seat, red-faced and gasping.

"What's happened? Is she all right?"

"She's coming out, Jamie. Let me get my breath back. I ran down three flights."

"When's she coming? Today?"

"Now. Give me a minute." So I had to wait while she puffed and blew for a bit. She seemed on the verge of a coronary. Finally, her breathing subsided.

"She's coming out now, Jamie. They're just signing her out. I've come down to collect her things." Mum had secreted a bag of Charlie's clothes in the boot against just such a moment.

"That's great, Mum. So she's okay?"

"Of course she is. She's much better." She wasn't listening, busy checking in her bag for her keys.

"But the doctors—what do they say?" I hadn't expected this—my heart was beating furiously, driven by excitement and anxiety.

"They say she's fine." A frown appeared on Mum's forehead as she looked up at me. "She's quite better. You saw for yourself yesterday. She's almost her old self again. Just very tired."

"Yes, but I mean, what about what happened—"

"She remembers it better now. There's no more of that nonsense. And listen, James, while we're on the subject—" Mum closed up her bag with a sharp click and leaned forward. "It's important that we're very careful with Charlotte for a while. The doctors say we mustn't talk about anything that could upset her. That means anything about Max or the funeral. I'll keep her off school for the moment too. She's easily disturbed at the moment, and we just want to help her get on with things slowly, all right?"

"But do they know why—"

"Promise me you'll help me out in this, Jamie. It's important."

"I promised that already, Mum."

"I know you did, sweetheart. It's going to be a difficult few weeks, dear, but we'll get along if we stick together as a family. The doctors will see her for a few checkups now and then. So it'll be fine. But remember what I've said, won't you?"

"Yes, Mum."

"Good boy." Mum levered herself out of the seat and turned back with her hand on the door. "You know, I think she's got over it a lot faster than they expected. She's a sensible girl, my daughter. I'd better run, sweetheart. We won't be long."

"Do you want me to wait here?"

But Mum had already slammed the door and raced around to the boot, where she retrieved the bag. Then she wheezed off again between the cars and was gone.

So that was that. I wasn't allowed to talk to her about any of it. I had to ignore it had ever happened.

A few checkups now and then. What did that mean? As I sat looking toward the glass doors, I found my heart was pounding against my chest, harder than ever. I drifted again. In my mind's eye, I saw her as she'd been the day before: watchful, reserved, answering the questions put to her and asking none. It was all very unlike the sister I knew and, now that she was coming home, I realized just how scared I was by what had happened—to her and not to me.

And here she was, almost at the car, and like a fool I hadn't noticed her coming.

Three

Prof. Sir. Peter Andover
Child Trauma Institute
St. Giles Hospital
London
WC1V 8EA

To: Dr A. E. Brown
Victoria Surgery
15 High View
Wrensham
WR13 7RT

Cc. Dr. David Tilbrook

20th September
My ref: FL1/1099
Your ref:
Re: Charlotte Fletcher

Dear Dr. Brown,

Thank you for your letter of the 16th September. As requested, I am writing to you with my immediate impressions of Charlotte Fletcher, whom I saw at Wrensham General Hospital last week.

Charlotte seems a bright, articulate, and personable girl. In ordinary circumstances I am sure she would be both truthful and precise in any accounts she gave. However, she is at present vague, hesitant, and suspicious of anyone taking interest in her story. From what she has said, to me and to others, I think we can divide her recollections of this tragic incident into two distinct phases, which are directly related to the responses of those she confided in.

1. Original story
I did not witness this directly, but I have been given a written summary by the doctor to whom Charlotte spoke when she arrived at hospital. In addition, I have talked with Charlotte's mother, to whom she gave her fullest original account. The response of the mother I take to be largely to blame for Charlotte's subsequent change of story.

You are well aware of the substance of her original claims. I would first say that accounts of this type—that is, ones of a fantastical and detailed nature—are by no means uncommon with trauma cases, nor with ones in which the patient has been near asphyxiation, as was the case here. To take the latter point first, restriction of blood supply to the brain often induces visual disturbance, which commonly consists of bright, disorientating colored lights, and more rarely, of prolonged dreamlike hallucinations. Such visions are commonly accompanied by intense physical sensations, which in retrospect often gives the memories a strongly "realistic" feel. If the circumstances of the sensations are highly unusual, as is tragically the case here, the patient may be easily convinced of their accuracy.

Turning to the former point, namely the circumstances of trauma. As you will no doubt be aware, intense shock and distress nearly always lead to the following chronological symptoms: denial, anger, and final acceptance. It is commonly the case with children that loss of a loved one that is actually witnessed can lead to some particularly strong "explanatory" fantasies, which at root seek to deny what has happened.

I think this is the case with Charlotte. It seems that after the boy fell in, she very bravely—her teacher says that she is an average swimmer, not a strong one—followed him into the pool. She was probably underwater for a long time, and may well have seen her friend below her, even if she could not reach him. The heroic effort that she made nearly cost her her life. In addition, those brief moments of oxygen starvation were combined with an almost insurmountable grief that she had been unable to save her friend. It is unsurprising then that her resulting memories of the event are confused.

I may say in passing that the notion of abduction of the deceased is not unknown, though it is unusual. It is an attempt to make sense of the senseless loss. It is true that some aspects of Charlotte's story are remarkably specific, e.g. the explanation of the slash on her leg, implying a strong analytical imagination.

2. Current situation
Although the doctor to whom she originally told her story had a modicum of training and refrained from passing judgment in any way, the girl also told her mother, who, perhaps understandably, was strongly disconcerted by the distressing combination of fantasy and tragedy. I think you will have observed that the girl's mother is neither diplomatic nor particularly sensitive, and it is clear from what she says that she greeted Charlotte's story with obvious disbelief.

Charlotte, who is an intelligent girl, and who was almost certainly aware of the incredible nature of her story, has subsequently refused to repeat it to anyone. When the police interviewed her, and later in a private talk with me, she was deliberately vague. The only details she gave of the event were these:

1. Her friend was playing in the tree.
2. He fell in.
3. She went in after him.
4. She saw him below her in the water, but could not reach him.

Although these are reasonable enough statements, and may confirm to what actually happened, she presented them with a singular clarity and a surprising lack of emotion. I suspect they were calculatingly presented in an effort to tell us what we "wanted" and rid herself of us as quickly as possible. Whether she believes this version is doubtful.

Analysis:
Although Charlotte may have rejected her false memory and reached a more accurate account of the event, it is more probable that she has suppressed it following her mother's skeptical response. She should be monitored closely over the next few months. Specifically, regular psychiatric counseling should be employed to ensure that she gradually comes to accept the truth. Great care and tact is required and the dangers Charlotte faces should be made known to those close to her. I am confident, however, that her visits to Dr. Tilbrook will help her gradually to come to terms with her tragic loss.

A full report will follow in due course. In the meantime, if I can be of any further assistance, please let me know.

Yours etc.

Peter Andover

Four

The staring irritated me a little. I got a taste of it straight away from Mrs. Mortimer next door, whose sixth sense told her precisely when we'd be back. She was hovering just over the wall, busily testing her washing with her big thumbs, though anyone could see it was bone dry. All the while we were getting out of the car she had her back to us, but then, as I walked up to the door, she got a good look in, swiveling her neck right round like an owl. I heard her clucking away with ostentatious pity as James fumbled with the keys. Mum was red-faced and flustered as she ushered us inside. From then on, whenever I ventured into the yard, Mrs. Mortimer was always somewhere in shot, peering through her windows as she cleaned them, or picking her runner beans while looking at me out of the corner of her eye.

If Mrs. Mortimer was persistent, the kids down our street were louder. Fat-boy Larson and his mates turned up in the back alley on the second morning I'd been back, balancing on their pedals and whispering. I was going to the shops and had to pass them, but as I headed up they whooped and screamed with shrill false fear and sprinted away laughing. Snivvens called out a few things over his shoulder, which I only half heard. I went on walking, but James, who was in our yard, heard it too. When I came back an hour or so later, he was in the kitchen bathing a cut lip.

"What's up with you?"

"Walked into a door," he said, and went on dabbing. We didn't mention it again, but I knew he'd gone looking for Fat-boy and Snivvens.

Maybe the thing that got to him was that they had mentioned Max. To James, their words probably seemed an obscenity and a direct assault on me. But in truth, I had barely registered them; it was as if their shouts came from a far distance.

At that time, everything seemed like that—distant, padded and muffled somehow. Even my house was affected. When I first got back, I went straight up to what I remembered was my room and sat on the bed looking at the posters, the silly lampshade, the old faded carpet, and the books piled high on the little shelf. It was like when you come back from a long holiday, and for a few minutes you see the house as a stranger would see it, all unfamiliar colors and haphazard objects. But this time I could not make it fade back into comfortable familiarity. Everything stayed just that little bit different, alien, untouchable. The books and games stacked in the corner seemed the possessions of another.

Worse than this, a thick veil was over my eyes and I could not see Max anywhere. It seemed that the massive, unspoken certainty of everyone around me that Max was gone forever pressed down upon me every minute of the day. I had its heaviness when I awoke, when I lay down to sleep, and in every unappetizing minute of activity that filled the hours between.

Not once, except for those gleeful boys running down the alley, did anyone refer directly to him. And I was no better than they were, for the assumption about his fate that everyone silently imposed upon me almost snuffed out my memories of the pool. The images that I had replayed time and again on the hospital night screen flickered and dimmed. They became less close, less insistent, though not less real.

As the commonly held view closed itself around me, it sealed Max off. I could not think about him directly, nor the pool, nor the green-eyed women who had stolen him away. My mind shut it all out amid the tedium of life back home. But I see now that Max was always there, just out of vision, like that group of stars Dad used to point out to us when we were small, that mazy cluster that smudges into nothing when you look at it head on, but that flares into individual pinpricks of light when you look away. Max was always waiting, just beyond the edge, and everything I tried to do then was in his shadow.

* * *

All this is clear to me now. But in those early days, before the dreams began, I lost my way completely. I was listless and sapped of strength. Everything I did seemed pointless. I tried reading some of my old favorites, but their pleasures turned to dust on the page. Even *Treasure Island* and *Tales of Arthur* were dull. I found myself often just lying on the bed, with a book open on my lap, thinking of nothing.

I would have gone out a lot more, but during my week in hospital the weather had changed. The last remnants of summer vanished; it was cold and wet. A persistent drizzle fell on the town, forcing me to spend a lot of time indoors, rubbing up continually against my mum and brother.

James was trying so hard to be considerate it was painful. He went so far out of his way to keep everything light and trivial that I just wanted to scream. He offered to play snooker more often in three days than he had done in the previous three years. Other hitherto unknown things on his itinerary were taking me to the cinema, playing rubbish old board games we hadn't looked at for years, and wandering into my room aimlessly to see how I was getting on. I played a few games, but usually I just wasn't on for company. I couldn't summon the energy to tell him to get lost either, so one way or another he was always hanging around.

Mum's instinct was to stay well clear. We've never got on brilliantly and she knew she was treading on eggshells even more than normal now. I attempted to avoid her as much as possible, keeping to my room while she was downstairs watching telly. She rarely intruded, except for the first evening I was back. I was sitting on my bed, not doing much, when she stuck her head around the door.

"Can I come in?"

"You're half in already, Mum."

She came over and sat on the far edge of the bed. "How are you doing?"

"I'm fine."

"You don't have to stay up here. Why don't you come down? There's a good film on."

"I'm all right, Mum. Don't worry about it."

"Well—" She cast about for something else to say and hit on it with relief. "I spoke to Mr. Drover today, about you missing school. There's no problem; he's fine with you taking a bit of time off. He sends his best wishes. The whole school does. I told him you'd got the card. It's nice that they're all thinking of you."

Yeah, nice. Everyone in the class signed their love. Including Snivvens.

I gave Mum a special nonsmile. She plowed on.

"I don't think you need to be off for long, but I don't want you to get bored. There are lots of things we can do to keep busy. We could go on day trips."

"You'll be at work, Mum."

"I've taken another week off, sweetheart. After that, well, we'll see. It's only part-time anyway, so we'll have plenty of opportunity to do things."

"You don't need to do that, Mum." She hardly gets any holiday as it is. "I'll be fine. I can go out."

I was feeling okay toward Mum at that point, but then she went ahead and ruined it again. Her voice stiffened. "I'm not having you wandering the streets on your own, Charlotte. That's final. We can do lots of things together, and with James, too. And Greg's offered to let us all come over at weekends, if we want. There's plenty to do."

"Whatever." I'd lost interest again and was looking out of the window.

Ordinarily, Mum's words would have made me furious. I'd go where I pleased. She wasn't going to keep me on a leash and there was no way in hell I'd spend a weekend with Greg and his disgusting son. He's Mum's new bloke. Greg, I mean, not the son. But I couldn't summon up the energy to be angry. What was the point?

"I'm a bit tired, Mum," I said. "I might have a sleep."

"All right, dear." She got up heavily. I rolled over, facing away to the window, but I could hear her pause at the door. "Charlotte, love, if you ever want to talk about anything, you know I'll always listen."

She waited for an answer, but I'd already closed my eyes and was looking into a blank green haze. In the distance, I could hear the door shut softly.

On the Thursday after I got home, I visited the doctor's for the first time. It was on the other side of town, a big house in a leafy street. I'd expected a surgery, but it seemed to be Dr. Tilbrook's own place. He opened the door himself and showed us in to his lounge, filled with lousy black furniture and a few magazines on a coffee table. Mum had to wait there. I was taken through to the next room, which was his study. I sat in a comfy chair and he sat opposite. There were Athena prints on the wall behind him and beyond the patio doors a long unkempt garden stretched away.

"Hi, Charlotte," Dr. Tilbrook said.

"Hi," I said.

I looked at him with what I hoped was an open co-operative look. My plan was the same as ever—to be as reasonable as possible and get out quick. Even then, when I was still pretty stupid and shaken up and had lost Max from view, I knew what they were trying to push on me.

"It's a pleasure to meet you, Charlotte," Dr. Tilbrook said. He paused. An acknowledgment was required.

"Thanks," I said.

He was very tall and beany, so that he folded himself rather than sat in the chair. He seemed quite young, except for little wrinkles around the eyes, and he had a big mop of floppy hair with a hanging fringe, which every now and then drooped forward so far it looked like it would cover his eyes. He had the habit of flicking it back into place with a little shake of his head and never once moving his long thin hands, which lay out flat in his folded lap.

"I'm sorry about your loss," he said. "I heard what happened."

Of course you did, I thought. What a stupid thing to say. Why else would I be here?

"I'm here for you to talk to," he went on. "That's all. The

doctors who looked after you at the hospital thought that it would be good if you had someone who could listen, if you wanted to talk about things. There's nothing more to it than that. I'm just here to listen."

He paused. I didn't give him anything to listen to. I found I had a sudden urge to turn my head away from him and look out at the garden. I could just see it out of the corner of my eye. Green trees, long grass, and a slab of silvery gray that might have been a long, low rock or even a pond. But I knew that the more I cooperated the quicker things would be. So I smiled vaguely at him.

"How are you feeling at the moment, Charlotte?" Dr. Tilbrook asked. He never took his eyes off me.

"Fine," I said. "You know."

"Well, I don't think I do know really. You've had an experience that none of us can imagine—your mother, your brother, or me. But you mustn't feel that you're alone. We're all wanting to reach out and help, every one of us. In fact, everyone you meet, everyone who knows about it, will want to help you if they can. You mustn't forget that."

I thought about Snivvens and Fat-boy. I smiled vaguely again.

"Do you feel you can talk about it at all, Charlotte? Have you chatted to anyone?"

The itch to look out into the garden was terrible now and I didn't want to look at his face either. I compromised by looking at his flowery tie, hanging down low above his long still hands.

"I've told people what happened," I said. This was true. In fact I'd told people a couple of different versions, but I wasn't about to tell them again to him.

"I know it is difficult to talk," he said. "You shouldn't worry about that. But you shouldn't bottle things up either."

I shrugged. "I'm fine."

"Look, Charlotte." Dr. Tilbrook stretched out a long, thin arm, further than you'd think possible. He opened a drawer in his desk and pulled out a small book with a red binding. "You don't have to talk to me if you don't want to. We'll meet again next week and maybe you'll want to then. But there's something you might wish to do if you feel like it. And that's write things down, when they occur to you. Do you write a diary?"

I shook my head. Nope. Except sometimes for school. Dr. Tilbrook nodded.

"I don't either. But I do sometimes make notes of things, when they're important and I want to remember them. I use a special notebook. Blank, like this one. Take it, if you like. If you feel something's inside you and has got to be said, write it down here. No one else will read it, but it's good to get things off your chest."

He reached over and handed me the book. "Thanks," I said. I didn't open it.

"Right. Well, it was nice to meet you. I'll see you again soon."

He unfolded himself and went to the door. As I went out, I allowed myself a quick glance at the garden. The sun was lighting up the leaves and I saw that the gray slab of color was a stone in a rockery beside a path that led off under the trees. It was a pretty garden and I had a sudden desire to break off and walk up the path on my own, but the door Dr. Tilbrook opened for me led off to the front, to Mum, the car, and the road.

Five

I was treading through long damp grass, barefoot. With every step, new stipples of wetness prickled my toes and the sides of my feet. Directly above me, the sky was a deep blue, darkening into night, but to left and right both sky and grass faded quickly into nothingness. I was walking along a narrowing strip toward a single spotlit point.

What was at that point? Nothing but a dark, still circle, lying in the grass. I knew it for what it was: the pool, just as I remembered it, in every detail. The fringe of stone, the shadow of the trees, the motionless water waiting.

I walked and walked, and though I seemed to see the pool more clearly with every step, so that soon I could pick out the individual cracks in every stone, see the smears of mold and lichen gumming up the joins between, still I felt myself no nearer to it. A great anxiety swelled in me; a terrible urge to reach the water before something dreadful and very imminent happened. But I could not increase my pace, no matter how I tried.

And then he was there, standing in the water, with only his feet and ankles hidden, for all the world as if it were as shallow as a baby's paddling tub. He was as still as stone; with his arms hanging loosely and his head cocked slightly to one side, he and the water could both have been carved from a single piece of marble, so motionless were they. And though I was far off, I could see every line and contour of his pale, pale face, and the living eyes looking at me.

Then, just as he opened his mouth to speak to me, the pool sucked him down. His hair billowed briefly like fronds upon the surface and was gone.

With one great effort, I wrenched myself forward. I was beside the pool, looking into the opaque waters. I could see nothing, but I knew he was there below me, close enough to touch, with his arms outstretched toward the air. I strained my eyes to either side, in case the enemy was waiting, but nothing was visible at all.

The green waters waited.

And so, without even pausing to draw breath—

I leaped.

Six

Charlie gave us our first shock that morning. It was Saturday, around eleven o'clock and she still hadn't turned up for breakfast. Mum started prowling round the kitchen, pointedly removing various items from the table until only the bare minimum bowl, mug, and spoon were left with a token packet of cereal. The old Mum would have got tetchy much earlier, but these days she and I were both on our best nonirritable behavior. As eleven o'clock came and went and Charlie still didn't appear, I volunteered to put my head round her door and give her a friendly prod.

She was gone. Her bed was rumpled and slept in, but it was now Charlie-less, and her trainers and coat weren't obvious either. Something sharp jabbed into my intestines as I pelted downstairs and shouted to Mum.

"She's gone! She's not in her room."

Mum's face seemed to cave in with worry, as if someone had pulled a support out from under the skin. "Don't,

James—you're frightening me. She'll be in the bathroom. Did you look there?"

"She's not in the bathroom, Mum. The door was open."

"But did you look?"

"No! All right, I'll look—but she isn't." I pounded up the stairs and looked, and of course she wasn't. Or in Mum's or my room either. I ran back down, and straight out the back. Charlie's bike was gone from the shed. Mum's anxiety morphed into a series of unanswerable questions.

"When did she go? How did she slip out? How long have you been awake? I thought you were keeping an eye on her."

"How the hell do I know where she is? I thought I heard her when I came down for breakfast—but that was two hours ago. She could be anywhere. Shut up and think for a minute."

We stood either side of the kitchen table, neither of us able to sit down. Between us sat the forlorn and lonely packet of Rice Krispies and the tidy, empty bowl. I stood there thinking. Since she'd come back, she'd not gone out much on her own—down the shops a couple of times, perhaps—and each time she'd told Mum where she was going. This felt different. She must have gone out really early, before either of us was awake.

"It's no good," Mum said. "She could be anywhere—stop doing that!" I was drumming my fingers on the sink cupboard door. Mum was rubbing the side of her face, as she does when she's really upset. It's been red and sore for days now. I stopped drumming. A really horrid thought had struck me.

"Mum, you don't think she'll have gone back, do you?"

"God, James, how can you say that? She'd never go back, never. . . ." Mum broke off and looked me in the eye. I didn't say anything.

We were out of the house and into the car in thirty seconds, and that was including me going back to slam the front door, which Mum had left open. She turned the key in the ignition, and the engine failed. Mum pulled out the choke too far and flooded it. She swore. She tried again. It ground and growled. The car was hot and stuffy. A stench of panic hung in the air. On the third time, the engine started. Mum sat back as she pulled out of the drive, and I realized we had both been bolt upright in our seats, rigid at the delay.

Neither of us said anything on the journey out of town. I was busy figuring out the route Charlie might have taken—along the canal path and down onto the B-road behind Sainsbury's. Took you to within a mile of Bingham, and from there it was only another mile or so to the mill. I reckoned Charlie could have done it in an hour, door to door. Try as I might, I couldn't think of anything that would have held her up. Even if she'd dawdled, she'd have been there well over an hour before us, minimum. *An hour at the pool.* Christ! I suppose Mum was thinking similar things. She didn't drive well and nearly mowed down one deaf old boy who tried a bit of jaywalking.

We got to Bingham in fifteen minutes, and shot up the lane to the mill, screeching to a halt by the main gate. I was out before the car stopped, and began pelting up the path toward the millstream, leaving Mum to follow along behind. I pounded over a cattle grid, and saw, beyond the field, a fringe of trees. I knew what they were. It was still some distance away, but you'd see if anyone was standing there, and there wasn't.

I vaulted the fence and ran over the field, skidding in at least one fresh cow turd on the way. Halfway across, I began to see—here and there on the trunks of a few trees—little bright scraps of plastic tape that the police had forgotten to remove. I felt sick. Far behind sounded snatched coughs and Mum's faltering footfalls. I clambered over the barbed wire at the other end, snagging my jeans en route, and staggered to a standstill beside the pool. My breathing was as ragged as my jeans.

The pool had been covered over. A rough platform of wooden boards, obviously cobbled together from anything available, had been laid out across the entire circular surface of the pool. It was bolted down with giant rivets, which fixed the end of each board to the solid stone beneath. It was some feat to do the whole thing that way—it was a big area—but you couldn't see one bit of water. The millstream ran under the boards at one side, and ran out again at the other, and at both places a metal grille, securely fixed, hung down into the sluggish water. The whole thing was very ugly and extremely secure.

Thank God for that. Even if she had come, she'd have been unable . . . well, the bloody thing was closed over and that was enough.

I turned to watch Mum negotiating the far fence, and then I saw Charlie, sitting hunched and hidden in the shadow of the nearest plum tree, staring at the boards.

She was crouched low and her hair hung over her eyes so that you couldn't see them. Her arms were clasped around her knees and her chin rested on top. She made absolutely no sign at all that she had seen me, her big brother, coming racing over the fields like a fool after her. All around her was a mess of torn flowers and plastic wrapping. The petals were scattered like confetti and the stalks were ripped and weeping.

"Charlie." I went over to her. "Charlie?"

She made an "mmph" sound into her knees. I didn't know what to say. Savaged flower heads lay all around.

"Are you okay?" No answer to that. She didn't look up, just stared straight ahead through tangles of hair at the hideous boards.

"Come on, Charlie. It's me. Mum's here too."

"Great." That was a good sign. She sounded a little like her grumpy old self again.

"Come on," I said again. "How long have you been here?"

"I don't know. Not long."

"What's all these flowers, Charls?"

"James! Is she there?" I peered round the side of the

plum tree. Mum was approaching the near fence. She had given up running and was looking uncertain at the prospect of mounting the wire.

"Yeah. Everything's fine, Mum. Come back with us, Charlie. Where's the bike?"

"Look, I'm just sitting, all right? Just leave me in peace, okay?"

"Well, we were worried. You should have told us where you were going."

"Yeah right, and you'd have let me go, would you? All right—I'm coming now. I don't want Mum to cause a scene here." Muffled curses were coming from the fence.

That wasn't fair on Mum, really—even Charlie must have known that. But I sort of saw what she meant. There was a gray solemnity about the spot that would go out of the window if Mum and Charlie started arguing.

"I'll help you up then." I stretched out a hand. Unexpectedly, Charlie took it. Her nails and fingers were stained green up to the second knuckle.

She got up stiffly. Mum was over the fence now, and I put my arm round Charlie and led her over. I was keen to prevent Mum seeing the massacred flowers.

"Charlie!" Mum enfolded her. "We've been worried sick, sweetheart."

Charlie was quite passive. "I'm okay, Mum. My bike's behind that tree."

We collected the bike and wheeled it back to the car. All the way home, Mum chattered on gamely about nothing much, having enough sense to keep off the morning's events. Charlie sat beside her, saying nothing. I was in the back, with the mucky bike wheel pressing against my neck from behind, thinking about the shredded flowers. I could just see Charlie's spattered hands resting demurely in her lap.

After lunch, Mum went out. I suspected she was gone to get advice. Charlie and I stayed in and watched a crap western. By now, she had washed the evidence away.

Finally, while the rancher was arguing woodenly with some other two-bit actor, I said, "What were those flowers, Charlie?"

"What flowers?" She didn't look at me.

"Did you bring them?"

"Of course not."

"So they might have been from his—"

"His mum or dad, or teacher or whatever. I don't know. It certainly wasn't me, laying them out so prettily on the side there. Bloody pathetic they looked."

"But you shouldn't have touched them, Charls! You know that." I thought of the funeral and how Max's mum and dad had looked then.

"You put flowers down for a bloody road accident or something. Not for this."

"Charlie—"

"Not for Max. Not like that. And they shouldn't have covered it either."

"They want it to be safe, Charlie."

"Yeah, right. They want to cut him off. Wooden coffin boards and funeral flowers. I can't stand it. I'd have torn up the cover if it wasn't so bloody well nailed down."

"So why did you go back?"

She didn't answer me, but just stared at the TV, watching three Hollywood rejects slug it out with blanks across a studio lot. I very badly wanted an answer, but I knew I shouldn't push her. Also, I was a little afraid of the answer she wasn't giving me. I thought I could guess what she might say. What her pale impassive face was keeping secret. That she had gone back to the pool for Max, and that if she'd not seen him among the fronds, or maybe even if she had, she'd have kicked off her shoes and slipped herself down into the cold dark water to try and bring him back.

We sat in the sitting room watching bad television, neither of us choosing to leave. She sat staring into the screen like she could see something beyond it, and I sat looking at the side of her face, wishing I could fathom something behind that surface too.

Seven

At first, I hoped that Max would return to me as I slept the following night, and would help to guide me. But for several days I did not dream again.

So they had closed him off. From the moment when I saw the barrier, a great despair rose up in me, a terrible sapping lethargy that filled every waking hour, which clung to me as I slept and in the morning was renewed. The dreary weight of that one simple fact bore down on me at all times. Max was gone and the entrance was barred. I could not follow him.

James had been unsettled by what had happened and pestered me for a reason. I had nothing to say to him even if I had wanted to. Mum was shaken up too. She still didn't go back to work, and began to spend even more time trying to keep me occupied, loitering in my room and driving me mad with bright suggestions. At her insistence, I was taken round to Dr. Tilbrook's for an extra appointment, and found him much more decisive than before. He made me tell him all over again about Max and asked me what I thought of it. I said I was sorry he was lost and he seemed a little cheered by this. I think he took it the wrong way.

But I was lost too. I had no idea what I should do next.

Mum didn't let me out much on my own, but I spent a lot of time thinking about the things Max and I had done. A couple of days later, when Mum was out and James at school, I seized my chance and cycled off. I didn't head far, just to the old haunts around town, tracing out our favorite routes, that kind of thing.

Our area is quite good for cycling, but you have to know the back ways. All around the place, there's a network of narrow terraces stretching up and down between the park and the canal. All the houses have tiny yards behind them, and all of these have gates at the end leading on to cobbled alleys. These alleys are good for speed, with the extra interest that comes from unexpected obstacles: raised cobblestones, slalomed parked cars, women hanging out washing, and small kids who are tired of life coming out of gates without looking. There's also the advantage that you avoid most traffic, especially the main overpass system a few blocks away. There are roundabouts and dual carriageways there that would be certain death to cycle on. Max had done it once, for a dare.

If you burn through the alleys, heading downhill, you eventually pass out into the allotments where the old men grow cabbages and weeds. There are good routes here too, if you're quick enough to avoid the old codgers hidden among the pea canes. Beyond all this are the factories and the canal.

I put on the brakes at the old steel factory. This was one of our chief delights, Max and I. They'd shut it when I was little, maybe before I was born, taking the soul out of the town, Mum says. A lot of men who were young then now work at the new car place by the motorway, but some of the older ones didn't find jobs, and still hang about in the pubs on the corners of our streets. The factory was something to do with the old steel industry. Lots of hefty equipment is still out rusting in the rain more than ten years later. They put barbed wire on the walls and shut it up, but Max and I knew how to get in all right. We had a secret entrance at a gate where the metal sheets were loose.

I pushed the bike between the rusty sheets and squeezed in after it. Everything was the same. The weeds were growing up through the cracked concrete and the big stained metal husk of the old loading bay was still there on the right, unchanged. It was a while since we'd been, but there were plenty of memories to make my eyes prickle.

The steelworks was a great place for dares. There were some cranes to climb and a couple of man-made concrete-sided pit things that would kill you if you fell in. Don't know what they're for. Maybe they had machinery in once. Between us, Max and I had climbed most of the cranes, and skirted both the pits, holding on to the rails on the inside.

I left the bike by the fence and walked across to the

nearest crane, which we'd guessed had been used to load lorries. Its basic shape was still firm, but the rain had contorted the iron surface into lava flows of orange-reds and browns.

I sat on the metal base. On our first trip here, Max had climbed halfway up it, egged on by me. He'd got his shirt and jeans smeared with rust, and had a wallop from his dad for it later. After he got down, I'd climbed it too, to show I wasn't beaten. I could match him every time for climbing, running, whatever we did. But it had been Max who'd gone up first. It was the same story, almost always: Max leading, me following. Now I was here alone for the first time, smelling the rust and the damp and hearing the scuffling of rats under the hollow platforms. The sun was up; it warmed me where I sat, but I felt an emptiness in me, reflecting the desolation all around.

He was gone. Wherever he was, he was not in this place, where he had once been so strongly. I knew that now the decaying factory utterly lacked the life that we had given it before, when Max and I were there together.

He was far away, and I remained behind, purposeless.

Eight

But now consciousness comes. It grows like a seed in the earth, spreading slowly from the center outward, and I become aware of my head and its position. I am lying on one side, with my eyes closed and my mouth open. My nostrils are painful with the smell of salt. My cheek rests on something wet, rough, granular; and somewhere close I hear the crashing of the sea.

I cannot open my eyes: something gums them shut. My tongue is dry, my lips salted over with a crust which shatters when I close my mouth. I try to flex my fingers, they are stiff with salt, and ache as if they haven't stirred for days.

One arm is trapped under my body. I raise the other, and hear the salted surface of my clothing crack. I lift my fingers to an eye and rub away at the crust that seals the socket until I can open the lid halfway. I can see nothing. It is quite dark around me. Close by, the sea breaks against the shore. I run my hand over the side of my chest and stomach and feel a shower of dry flakes fall off me on to the sand. I am covered all over with a coating of sea salt, as if I have been dead and floating for days.

The rhythm of the waves lulls me. My arm falls back against the sand.

Consciousness fades.

The seed dies.

Nine

There was something in that dream which made me change. Nothing precise, you understand. I couldn't tell you what it was about that moment when I sat up in bed with sleep crusts in my eyes and the smell of sea salt in my nose that altered me forever. It was only that I had awoken with such a pressure in my chest that if I didn't do something about it then and there I felt I would burst.

For a week or more, since I had seen Max in the pool, my sleep had been empty. Now I dreamed again, and strange though the dream was, it galvanized me, haunted me throughout that day. In the mornings following, I woke up with the strongest sensation that I had dreamed it again, or something very similar, but I could grasp nothing except the nagging imprint of a fading intensity.

I felt an urge inside me, an inexplicable eagerness to know more—quite unlike any other feelings I had at the time. It injected me with more real emotion than anything else could, and the frustration of losing the images stayed with me all day long. Quickly, I began to cast about for a way of fixing the memory of my dreams in place.

All this time the notebook that Dr. Tilbrook had given me to record things was sitting unused on the shelf where it had been tossed. I had a distaste for his gift, which made me disinclined to touch it, but it gave me an idea.

I remembered that dreams are often in your head the moment you wake up, but that they fragment and fade almost immediately. The answer had to be to record them as quickly as possible, and that meant pen and paper.

Beside my bed was a small cabinet. I kept stuff there. Keepsakes and rubbish jewelry, things like that. It was all junk and no one but me could have any interest in any of it, not even James.

But the cabinet had a false bottom. It was a loose plank really. You could lift it up and see a hollow space above the carpet. I used it as a secret compartment in the days when James and I were always at war. Two of the things Dad gave me were there—a penknife from Switzerland and a walnut box with a moving plastic bug. I never looked at them now, although I'd carried the knife around a lot after Dad left.

I found a pen and an old cheap notebook with thin rules, and hid them both in the compartment. My plan was this. Every night, before I slept, I would get the book out and put it on the cabinet beside me. Then, as soon as I woke, I would write down any details I remembered before I could forget.

I tried it the next morning. And though I could hardly hold the pen in my sleepy fingers and barely open my eyes to see the page, it worked—in a small way. This was how my diary began.

Wednesday
Darkness around me. I am sitting on a beach. I feel sickness. The smell of salt is all over me. I can't brush it off.

That was all I got down. I wasn't practiced at fixing the details yet. But I could see the dream was very like the ones of the nights before. I tried again the next morning, and this is what I got.

Thursday
The sun rises over the sea. I am still sitting there, looking out at the horizon. The sickness is less. The salt smell clings to me, though I am no longer covered.

In the next night's dream I was walking on the beach, slow and hesitant, looking around. Each time I dreamed, the details got clearer and my writing got easier. I seemed to wake the moment each one finished, and if I wrote quickly I always got something down.

These were no ordinary dreams. They connected for a start, and they were more real to me than anything in the day. But it was the next night that showed me truly what they were.

Saturday

I was standing a couple of paces from where the waves lapped. The tide was going out and the sand around was still very wet. And I could see footprints. They came out of the sea and headed off inland in a dead-straight line.

I bent down to the nearest print. It was crisscrossed with lines and had an oval imprint in the heel. Crouching there, I bit my lip until it bled: Max's Nike trainers had that pattern on the sole. Before I straightened, a vague dread made me scan the sand for a few yards on either side of Max's trail, but there was no sign that anyone else accompanied him.

So I began to run, following the trail, my feet making bigger strides than Max had done. He must have been walking, slowly, leisurely, hesitantly? But he had never once turned around that I could see, never once looked back. I longed to catch sight of him somewhere ahead, to shout and make him turn.

It was impossible to make out where I ran. The sun was setting straight ahead. It blazed like a furnace; from its white heart yellow-red flames licked out to consume the horizon. It would have blinded me if I had looked up, but I had eyes only for the ground, for the prints flashing beneath my feet.

The sand moved under me unchanging. My heart was bursting in my chest. I was gasping, panting, straining with the effort.

I panicked. I admit it. I threw all my energy into calling out, hoping against hope that he would hear me. I shouted his name out loud—and woke up.

I was in bed, on my side, one leg forward, one leg back, with my duvet tightly strung between them. I was drenched with cold sweat. My toes were clawed into the sheeting, and my heart was going so hard my body shook with it.

I could hardly wait for the next night. Now I knew why the dreams had affected me so strongly. Max was in them. He was there—and not a memory of him either, but a living, moving Max, the Max I'd lost. If I followed, I could find him. It was strange, but it took no time at all for me to realize that what I saw in these dreams was real. I had leaped in after him. I was close behind. And somewhere up ahead was the friend that had been taken from me. Somewhere up ahead, Max was still alive.

Sunday
I was among tall grasses, on the top of a high dune. The waves murmured in the distance behind me. I was bent forward, scanning the ground at my feet, but the sand between the clumps of razor grass was bone dry and as I took each step my own prints instantly collapsed to nothing. I felt a great weariness, but then a gentle wind blew up, soft against my face, and I was refreshed. I began walking through the sharp grasses, away from the sea.

Monday
Still walking. The grasses had gone, and the sky above was a bright blue. The ground was orange-brown dirt, baked hard. It stretched all around, out to the horizon. No prints.

For the next three nights my dreams did not alter. I walked in that endless expanse of orange earth. The sun was always high and the sky was always blue. Nothing happened. I saw no one. I wrote little. At last, during the third dream, with the sky and earth and my feet going on one in front of the other just as they had been for three whole nights, I suddenly felt it falling on me all at once: the weight of that terrible isolation. A great bulging knot of panic rose up in my chest and I awoke.

On Friday I was a little nervous about going to sleep. I didn't want that dream again. It wasn't like you could wake up when you wanted to either. But I needn't have worried. That night, the dream changed.

In front of me was a high ridge of orange-yellow rock. It was a sandstone cliff, with jagged outcrops of soft rock erupting into the blue sky far above me. A little to my left was a cleft in the cliff, narrow, deep and smooth sided, and from it trickled a small stream, which idled its way into the desert and was swallowed up. There was a narrow gap between the stream and the side of the cleft, a ledge covered with wet sand. I started along it. It was so narrow that my right shoulder brushed against the rock of the cliff, dusting my shirt with sand.

Then I saw the footprints again. There they were, the same striations, the weird crisscrossing lines and oval on the heel. Max had told me once that the rounded lump on the heel was to give extra shock absorption when you ran fast. But he was still walking now with the same easy steady pace that he'd had on the beach.

I felt grim satisfaction—I'd followed him right across the desert without even knowing I was doing so. I set off up the gorge at an easy pace. No point running. He would still be a long way ahead.

The dream ended, like ordinary, false dreams do, with a sudden weakening of the image, and a kind of pull somewhere inside, lifting you out again. The gorge and the stream, and the footprints and cliff all receded suddenly at a great rate, and I was awake again and it was morning. I could hear Mum in the kitchen downstairs, with the radio on.

Ten

Charlie came down on time this morning. She looked okay, better than normal in fact, and I gave her a friendly wave over my egg. She sat down. I passed her the flakes and it all seemed to be going swimmingly. Then Mum put her foot in it again.

"How are you feeling, Charlie? You're all right, aren't you?"

I gave Mum a black look. She was in Concerned Mother mode, guaranteed to put Charlie's back up.

"I'm fine. Could you pass the milk, James?"

"Only I heard you calling out in the night."

"I'm not interested, Mum."

"I went to your door, and you were sleeping. I didn't like to wake you."

"I said I'm not interested."

"All right, I'm just concerned about you, dear." The

phone rang. Mum retreated to the other room. Charlie busied herself with the flakes. I toyed with the last scrap of toast, smearing vestiges of yolk around the plate.

"What are you up to today, Charlie?"

"Don't know. Might go out."

"Do you want to get the bikes out? I was thinking of going for a ride. Don't know where exactly." I didn't know because I had just made this up.

"Yeah. Maybe." That was vaguely promising. Normally I got the brush-off. I didn't push it. Charlie finished her flakes while I ate my toast and drank my tea, which was cold.

Mum reappeared. "That was Greg. He's invited us over for lunch, which is nice of him. I hadn't got much in and it saves us a shop this morning. Graham will be there too, so that'll be fun." She was talking too fast, like she always does when she tries to convince us about Greg. She's onto a loser on this, because the guy is tedium incarnate. He makes cutting your toenails seem interesting. And his son, Graham, is worse. A spotty games-obsessive with too much hair. Nasty. I wouldn't have wanted to see them even on a good day. Charlie and I both opened our mouths and Charlie got in first.

"So we're going, are we?"

"Well, I said yes, Charlotte. It'll be fun—"

"Can't you have the courtesy to ask if we want to go? James can if he wants, but I'm not. I'm going out."

"Charlotte, you know you shouldn't spend so much time on your own." Mum was getting twitchy again, rubbing at the side of her face. "I want to have you beside me. I worry about you."

"Well stay at home then. I'll stay in too, if that's what you want."

"But I promised Greg. It'll be good for you."

"No, Mum, it'll be good for *you*. You go."

"I think I'll stay here too, Mum," I said. "Charlie and I were thinking of going for a bike ride. We'll be fine." I was attempting a tricky one here, trying to convince Mum that all would be well, with me implicitly "looking after" Charlie, while at the same time not getting Charlie's back up. I don't often pull this kind of thing off. Usually, I get kind of squashed in an emotional sandwich, with both of them turning their fury round on me, but this time it worked. Mum rubbed her face a bit, then agreed, with minimal moaning. I think she was glad to get a trip out on her own. She'd been hanging around after Charlie for weeks without a break.

Charlie and I got the bikes out and wheeled them to the front of the drive.

"So, where do you want to go?" I said.

"Don't know. Just cycle. I'll follow."

We set off. I sailed on ahead, trying not to look around too often to see if Charlie was keeping up. The second time I peeked, she scowled and shouted something I couldn't catch, so I didn't try that any more.

We cut down through the allotments, toward the gray-brown mass of the factories. I passed the steelworks as fast as

I could. Charlie used to go there a lot with Max. Not good vibes. In five minutes we were coming out of the road with corrugated fencing and down a ramp onto the canal path. There's a sharp left turn there, onto the ramp, and I nearly mowed down an old lady who was pausing in my blind spot while her runt of a dog peed up a lamppost. I swerved at the last second, and looking back, saw the old dear jump like a jackrabbit as Charlie's bike motored round on an even tighter curve.

We followed the canal along the concrete towpath for a while, past the new estates and the brewery. Finally, I needed a rest and maybe a chat. I hadn't looked around since the ramp, so I could only assume that Charlie was still behind me. I braked, slowed and stopped. Immediately, I was nearly sent flying as Charlie's bike crashed headlong into mine. She toppled off and fell in the grass beside the towpath. I jagged my hand against the brake lever as I jerked forward. Nasty white scrape with the skin slightly torn.

"Watch it, you idiot!" My temper was strained, but it just about held.

"What did you stop so suddenly for?" Charlie was sullenly disentangling herself from the mess of wheel and metal.

"Just needed a rest. You weren't looking, were you?"

"I was following your back wheel. I was right on it."

"Idiot. You weren't thinking. You all right?"

"Of course."

She rubbed indifferently at a grass graze on her leg, then rolled over and looked out at the canal, where a lone duck was swimming aimlessly. All of a sudden, an anxiety hit me—what a fool I was!

"Charlie, sorry—the water, does it—"

"Does it what?"

"I didn't think about—you know . . ."

"Oh shut up about that. It doesn't bother me."

"Really?" I sat down next to her. "Oh. That's good." There were crisp packets and cans scattered in the long grass above the water, and something nasty festered nearby. It wasn't the best spot for a chat. "Do you want to move on?"

"I'm all right here."

Not the best spot, but perhaps it would do. Maybe, in a weird way, it was kind of appropriate. The duck floated past vacantly. I waited a moment, half hoping that something unexpected would happen to prevent me from asking her about it. Nothing did. I opened my mouth and began.

"Charls, you've got to be able to talk to me. You've got to trust me."

"What about?" Her voice was level, dulled; she could barely be bothered to speak, let alone add any life to it. She gazed out at the oily water.

"Look, don't think I'm going to go running to Mum or anything. You know me better than that. All I wanted to say was that you can talk to me about anything you want."

She smiled a little. "That's what they all say."

"Well, I've been meaning to say it since you were back. And it's true."

I paused. I knew I sounded lame. Charlie didn't even look around.

"Look. When Mum came home that first time, she told me what you'd said."

"I don't remember anything about it now. Just leave it, J, will you?"

"Well," I continued heavily, "I know that Mum reacted pretty strongly to what you said then. I won't do that, if you want to tell me. That's all."

Charlie scratched her leg intently and said nothing.

"I'm really sorry about Max," I said.

"So am I." There was no emotion in her voice, or in her eyes.

"I'm sorry that I didn't . . ."

"Get on with him? Don't worry about it. It's too late for that. He didn't like you much either."

Actually, I'd been going to say that I was sorry that I didn't get to know him better. But now Charlie had put it like that, I was kind of glad she'd interrupted. I wasn't being quite honest. When it came down to it, I *hadn't* much liked him, really. He was a bit too—I don't know—mindlessly energetic for me. Always racing about, never stopping to think. Sneaking into the factories, cutting school; I told myself that I was too mature for all that, but the truth is he made me feel a bit square. Charlie thought the world of him—and he liked her too of course. Didn't hang around with anyone else half so much, not even any of his mates. They were always going off together, Charlie and Max—and I got a fair bit of stick for that at school. But I hadn't realized he'd disliked me as well. Disliked by a dead kid. Don't know how that makes me feel.

I sat quiet for a bit, thinking this kind of thing. Charlie looked at me once or twice sidelong. Maybe she thought I was cut up about Max not liking me. Anyway, to my surprise, she broke the silence herself.

"It doesn't matter what you, or anyone else says, J. I feel quite alone, and I have done since I lost him."

"You're not alone, Charls! I know Mum drives you mad, but she's always there for you. And so am I."

"I don't mean that. I mean I've *lost* him—I'm looking, but I don't know where he is. And you can't help me."

"What—"

"It just makes me feel empty and alone. I know you and Mum and all the rest want to help, but you're all going about it the wrong way."

"What do you want us to do?"

"You're trying to distract me; you know, with games and trips out. Even this bike ride—it's just a diversion to keep me occupied, and not thinking of Max."

"Actually, I was trying to save you from Greg."

"Yeah. Well, fair enough. That worked." A small smile, the first I'd seen for a long while. I laughed a bit, willing her to laugh too. She didn't, but her posture relaxed a little and, better than that, she carried on talking.

"I don't mind it because you're only doing what you think is right," she said. "You're trying to turn my attention to new things, because you think Max is dead and it would be healthy for me to look away and get on with stuff. I don't blame you. But it's just wrong, that's all."

Something she said unsettled me deeply. I tried to be tactful. "What should we be doing?"

"Just leaving me alone. I don't blame you, J. It's just that I can't ignore Max now. I can't leave him."

Can't? "But, Charls," I said, "you've got to . . . leave him sooner or later. I mean, he'd have wanted it that way." God, that was clichéd, but I was really struggling.

"No. That's just it. He doesn't want it that way, I'm sure of it." A hard edge had returned to her voice. She wasn't smiling any more.

"You make it sound like he's . . ." I broke off, knowing I was on dangerous ground, but my frustration was beginning to get the better of me. "The thing is, Charls—"

"I know what you're going to say, and don't say it. I think I'm going home now."

"But, Charls—"

"Don't say it. I've lost him for the moment, but I'm still looking. I'm on his trail. Don't try to make me give him up completely." She levered herself off the ground. "Well, I'm going now. I'll see you later."

I shouldn't have said it, but I did. A great panic had come over me, at the sight of my sister leaving, still bound to her dead friend. It was like he was right there, standing dripping at her shoulder and calling her to follow. She was going off with him, leaving me, alive, alone. I know it sounds stupid, but she'd really put the wind up me, with all those little hints. I suddenly left tact behind, desperately wanting her to acknowledge the single basic fact before she went. I shouldn't have said it though.

"Charls," I said, "Max is dead. You've got to accept it sometime. It's not your fault, but you've got to understand—he's dead. You can't find him any more."

"You're just like all the rest!" Blood flooded into her face, which simultaneously went white with rage. She lashed out at me with a foot and caught me on the thigh.

"Ow! Charlie!"

"Just leave me alone! I'll find him on my own!"

She seized her bicycle with a sudden violence, wrenching it up from the ground so savagely that the pedal gashed her ankle. She swore, hurled herself up onto the saddle, and was away up the towpath, leaving me to sink back among the grass and litter. I wouldn't have cared about her shouting—or kicking me—if only she'd acknowledged the truth of what I'd said, somehow.

Eleven

James and I gave no hint of the row when Mum got back. I went upstairs early and read *Tales of Arthur*, lying on my bed. I was so desperate for sleep that it took me till past two to drop off, and in the meantime I had to listen to James's snores through the wall. He never has trouble getting to sleep, and he also claims that he never dreams, which I don't believe.

Saturday
It was not what I had expected. I thought it would pick up in the sandstone gorge again. Instead I was in a well of greenness. For an instant, visions of the pool swam in front of my eyes, then I grew accustomed to the light and saw that this was a different kind of greenness to that of the water. It was lighter, richer, more alive. And there was a gentle sighing above me—the noise of wind moving through leaves. I was in a forest.

The first thing I did was get on my hands and knees and scan the ground for his tracks. But the ground was covered with a soft turf, scattered with twigs and leaves, and no footprint was to be seen. I straightened slowly. On either side, high ferns choked the spaces between thick trunks of oak and beech, heavily laden with summer leaves and moss. The light from above was filtered into a thousand shades of emerald. After the October dreariness of home this richness overwhelmed me.

An orange glint shone through the trees to my right: it was the sun striking the peaks of the sandstone ridge that I—and Max—had crossed by way of the gorge. I felt certain that Max's route had taken him into the forest and, looking around, I saw that there was indeed the merest suggestion of a track, a sinuous break between the ferns leading off among the trees. Without hesitation I took that way.

This was the most delightful stage of my journey so far. The sun's heat was kept at bay by the topmost leaves, and the air was light and scented with blossom. Thick clumps of brightly colored flowers erupted from each bank and scutterings from the undergrowth signaled the activities of small forest creatures, although they didn't come into view. I scanned the air for birds, but never saw a single one.

I walked for hours but didn't get weary. Once I came out on a high bluff and, between a natural frame of two tall silver birches, saw the forest stretching for miles all around. It faded into the blue distance until it blurred into the sky. There seemed no end to it.

Somewhere ahead of me is Max. He is down there, drawing me on. I feel it.

For many nights I walked through the forest. Around this time, I became more bothered than ever by James and Mum. No sooner was I awake than they were buzzing around me like flies, irritating me with irrelevant schemes. Would I come with them to the new Bishopsgate Center? We could shop and eat out, and maybe see a film. Would I come visiting cousin Lucy in Stretford? She was dying to see me. (Oops, wrong word, Mum! Embarrassment all around, except for me.) Would I like a coach trip to Bridlington? It would be great, not too crowded out of season and we could eat fish-and-chips down on the—

No! None of it, thank you! Leave me alone!

Except . . . some of their schemes had a good side: they knackered me out, ready for the evening. Nothing was worse than those nights when I was too excited to sleep, when my desire to enter the forest made me toss and turn and get more and more frustrated and finally stopped me from sleeping properly, so that I spent hardly any time there. So in the end I began to agree to many of my family's stupid plans, especially ones that involved physical exercise. Best of all was when James suggested going swimming. I agreed immediately and took to going to the pool with him almost every evening when he got back from school.

I also hoped the exercise would help me in my explorations of the forest. I found that I always woke up bone weary, with muscles aching after my long hours of walking, so I wanted to get as fit as I possibly could. All in all, I made the best of a bad lot. At least the dragging daytimes now had a worthwhile purpose.

However, for several weeks my dreams were barely worth recounting. I progressed still deeper into the endless forest and saw neither tracks nor any signs of life. Although still sure I was following Max's trail, I began to wish for something to break the monotony of the journey and became a little listless and depressed.

Then everything changed.

The path ran upward through the wood between thick clumps of dark trees. Boulders covered with lichen were piled up beside the steep, stony path. It was hard going, and my breath began to labor a little, almost for the first time since I entered the forest. Pretty soon, if I looked behind me, I could see across the tops of the trees to the horizon. The sun was low, and there was a reddish stain in the western sky.

Ahead of me rose a tall craggy rock face, naked at the top but with small gnarled bushes extending from crevices up and down its sides. The path angled right, circling the base of the crag, and soon it began to rise sharply, until my progress resembled the climbing of a steep staircase. On my left was the cliff wall, on my right, as the path rose above the level of the trees, an open gulf of tumbled rocks and scree.

At last, when it seemed that I must have circled the entire pinnacle of crag, the path suddenly ducked away into a fissure that split the rock in two, and adopting a more horizontal plane, wound its way between two cliff faces spotted with withered scrub. This ended abruptly on an open shelf covered with thin grass, which overlooked the forest.

For miles in all directions the endless olive-dark trees stretched. With the sun now setting, the whole western half of the forest was soaked with red, as if with a liquid fire. I shielded my eyes from the glare, and looked down on the trees, on dozens of distant glades, on narrow strips of land where the forest had fallen back. In one was a tall dim shape, shaded from the dying light, which might have been a rock similar to the one on which I stood, or perhaps a castle with turrets projecting out of it at many angles. In another, a great sheet of water lay calmly, reflecting dully the pale evening sky. In another . . .

There was a single strip of open land extending away to the north, so long and straight sided that it was almost a natural rectangle. It seemed fairly close to my crag, separated only by a narrow band of forest; at any rate, it was close enough for me to pick out a solitary figure moving northward across it, between the trees.

The figure was so far away, and the light was fading so quickly that it was hard to make out anything definite. But there was something about the short, slow stride and the hunched shoulders that told me I knew him.

"Max!"

I shouted my lungs out, there on that flat, grassy shelf at the top of the crag, as the red sun was drawn down into the trees and the light faded. My voice was swallowed by the evening air. The figure did not turn, but continued its steady progress, familiar and far off, until the glade and everything in it were swallowed by a blanket of reddish-tinged black. And I carried on shouting and shouting until the darkness spilt over the edges of the glade and enveloped the trees around it, and the stars came out overhead and echoed with my cries.

My voice ran out. I was hoarse with shouting. I gave up and lay down, and closed my eyes against the tears that welled up now that the possibility had gone. But there was a fierce feeling of defiance in me too, because I had seen him—I had seen the friend that everyone thought was dead.

Twelve

My cheeks and hands were still sticky with drying tears when I raised my head and saw that it was morning. Heavy rain pattered against the window behind the curtains. The light was poor, but my bedroom door was open and someone was standing in the room. It was my brother.

"What are you doing here?" I was bruised with sleep and could hardly make him out.

"I wondered if you were all right." There was a shiftiness in his voice. He was lying. "I thought I heard you crying out. Were you having nightmares?"

"No. What were you doing in my room?"

"I told you—"

"Oh get out." I'd had enough. I wanted to write down about Max—not that I was ever likely to forget it. James went, without arguing, which was another sign that he'd been lying. I picked up the open notebook lying ready on the cabinet. Had he seen it? Possibly. From now on, I would keep it in its hiding place at night, just in case my brother came snooping around again.

That Saturday could not go fast enough. It dragged on and on with a slowness that terrified me. In the afternoon I went to the cinema with a friend of mine from school. Alice had rung me a few days before and in a weak moment I'd agreed to go. How I regretted it now: I was far too distracted to talk much and Alice and I were sitting in silence even before the adverts started. Alice ate popcorn with a rhythmic action. I sat gazing at the darkened curtain, struck by an agonizing thought. It had never struck me before, but now I began to wonder exactly how time in the forest compared to time at home. Perhaps for every minute I spent awake, a minute passed in the forest too. If so, I was doomed. I would never catch up with Max. While I was here, dawdling through interminable hours with people I hardly knew, Max would be walking on, never pausing, never flinching, moving further and further away. I swear every second of that day was agony for me.

In the evening I went to the baths and swam forty lengths. I was determined to tire myself, so I jogged home too. Then I went to bed and tried to bore myself to sleep with one of Mum's flowery romantic books.

It took a while, of course. I wanted it too badly. And when at last I did sleep, and found myself on the crag, my worst fears were realized. The sun was high above the great expanse; many hours had passed since Max had walked the glade at dusk. With a heavy heart, I got to my feet and began

Northern Plains Public Library
Ault Colorado

to negotiate a way down to the forest floor. It took another wasted hour before I finally skidded to a stop at the bottom of the lowest scree. Then I set off slowly onward, in what I hoped was the right direction.

After a while, I came to a valley between two low hills, where towering trees stood set apart in rows. Their trunks were straight and bare right up to a great height, where their topmost branches spread out in soaring arches of foliage to meet each other and interlink. The sky was blocked out, and the sun's rays were turned a dim, dark green as they penetrated the canopy and drifted down to the grassy floor. The height and space and darkness of this place gave it a solemn, stately feeling, as if I were standing in a living cathedral, among great pillars of carved stone.

There were no ground plants here, and I could see a long distance in every direction, along each aisle of pillar trunks until they vanished in the green murk. I walked on for a time, and then, as I passed one giant trunk, I saw a flash of movement, far off in the dim shadows of the wood. It was away to my left, where the trees merged with the dark—a pale shape that moved behind a tree. With pounding heart and staring eyes, I stood quite still among the silent columns. My pulse beat in my temple, three times, four times, five, six . . . and then the shape appeared again, further off among the trees.

My feet made no noise as I crossed the green vault and ran along the next row of trunks, darting from the shadow of one tree to another. I drew closer to the moving shape; it was ahead of me and partly obscured by yet another aisle of trees and I could not be sure of its form. I darted silently across another open space to the next trunk and peered around.

It was a human figure, walking slowly away from me, its face concealed. My heart swelled in sudden hope and I opened my mouth to call—but at the last moment something made me pause. What was it? The green shadows made it hard to make out any details of the figure's clothes or features, but I felt it was too tall, too broad for the one I sought. The color too was odd; it showed up as a drab paleness gleaming amongst the shades. It was a discolored, dirty white all over, like faded paper or old chicken bones.

There was something disconcerting too about the way the figure moved. It went with a slow, regular tread that never faltered, never altered. Its head was slightly bowed, as if heavy with thought or weariness. Occasionally, I thought to hear a slight rustle as it brushed past a trunk or fern. Otherwise, it was entirely silent.

Consumed by doubt, I followed at some distance—not daring to get closer, yet reluctant to let the figure go. I did not want to approach it; I did not like its hanging hands and head. Its awkward strides reminded me of a sleepwalker's. And though its body was constantly brushed with the subtly altering shades of the wood, its head seemed permanently in shadow.

At last I decided to try and get a better look, to perhaps make out more clearly the walker's face or clothes. I did not want to leave it before I had learned something more: it was after all the only living creature I had seen in all my weeks of travel. So I speeded up a little, attempting to get alongside, while still keeping a good distance between us.

As quietly as possible I slipped from tree to tree, closer and closer to the figure. Now it was only ten paces away from me but, try as I might, I seemed unable to draw abreast with it, and in my frustration I paid no attention to the ground in front of me. I went faster still, and suddenly I put my foot down hard on a fallen branch, an old, dry limb that split in two with a crack like a gun going off.

The figure stopped dead. I froze where I stood.

Stiffly, it turned its head and looked at me.

I had been right. It was not Max.

It was a dead man's face, blank-eyed, sharp-boned, paper-skinned—looking at me.

I ran.

Down the nearest nave of trees, under the silent arches, across the dark grass, I ran with my lips drawn back, too terrified to scream. I ran and ran, hearing no pursuit, nor anything but the frantic patter of my footsteps falling. I ran till my legs gave out and I collapsed on my hands and knees in the middle of the grass, with my chest shuddering for air. I crouched there, breathing like a frightened animal, my eyes wide and shining in the gloom.

Then footsteps sounded right behind me, and I did not have the strength to rise.

Thirteen

I never brought up Max again. Nor did Charlie, and though I thought she would take a while to forgive me, in fact she acted as if our little chat had never happened. Even more amazingly, I began to notice in the next few days that she was getting more involved with life—especially things that got her out of the house and kept her busy. Mum was delighted and, on the days when she wasn't back at work, organized as many new trips and visits for Charlie as she could. I was pleased too, of course, but not as much as Mum. Something about my sister still bothered me.

In some ways, she did seem better. She didn't mope around so much and had far more energy. We went out together quite a bit at weekends and I thought Charlie had a new sense of purpose about her, which had to be healthier. Or so I tried to tell myself. But there was still a secretiveness about her; a nagging impression that she was hiding something under her calm exterior, nursing it, guarding it, letting no one else near.

Her nightmares gave me a clue. They began to come with increasing frequency, and often I would hear her crying out in her sleep. In the mornings she regularly looked ill and drained, as if she had worn herself out with bad dreams.

One morning I went into her room to try and calm her. She woke up and kicked me out, but not before I'd glimpsed a notebook on her bedside table, open with a pen resting in its fold. Later, when Charlie was in the bathroom, I put my head around the door, but the book was nowhere to be seen.

The fact that she'd removed it intrigued me. What was she writing in it? Whether or not it was anything important—anything to do with her thoughts, anxieties, beliefs about Max, whatever—I thought it was worth seeing for myself. Later that morning, when Charlie went out to the corner shop, I seized my chance. I looked in her cabinet, behind it, under the bed, under the mattress and in half her drawers, being desperately careful not to leave any brotherly traces. But my luck was out. Either she'd taken the book with her or she'd hidden it somewhere I couldn't fathom. For the moment, I had to give up.

That very afternoon, Charlie went out to the cinema with one of her mates from up the street. She hadn't been back to school since July, and had lost touch with her old gang. I don't think she'd seen that girl more than twice since the accident and they certainly didn't have much small talk when they met in the hall. But anyway, they headed off and, while she was out, Mum and I were paid a visit by Dr. Tilbrook, Charlie's shrink. It had all been arranged because Charlie was going out, and of course I hadn't been told anything about it.

"What's he coming over for?" I asked. I felt a bit defensive.

"He wants to talk to us about Charlotte, of course," said Mum. She was flustered. She didn't like the idea of him stirring things up, bringing bad news.

"Doesn't sound too good," I said. "Maybe he's baffled."

That hit a sore point. "Oh shut up, James. He was very upbeat on the phone. He said he's happy with the way things are going."

"Whatever you say, Mum."

"Well, try to be positive for heaven's sake. And sit up when he comes. He won't want to talk to you if you're slobbing about all over the furniture."

I wasn't disposed to talk to Dr. Tilbrook at all after this, but I'd already formed curiously mixed feelings about him. It's difficult to explain. I mean, I was sure it was good that Charlie was seeing him, and yet . . .

The thing is, whenever I saw her being driven off for an appointment, I always felt more anxiety for her than at any other time. For some reason, it was at those moments when all the feelings of annoyance I'd accumulated that day would peel off, and I would see Charlie quite simply as my little sister, alone and vulnerable. I don't know why. So anyway, I awaited the psychiatrist's arrival with an odd mixture of interest and reserve.

Dr. Tilbrook rolled up in a smart green car with a retractable roof. He was shown into the living room, with Mum seemingly on all sides of him at once. She ushered him into the best chair, the one opposite the sofa where I was nonchalantly lounging. He was a youngish bloke, tall and a bit too thin, with a mop of floppy hair and a lot of crow's feet around his eyes. I thought he'd be pale and unhealthily bookish, but his face was surprisingly tanned.

"Hi," Dr. Tilbrook said.

"Hello," said I.

Mum made a pot of tea for herself and me. Dr. Tilbrook took coffee. I was lounging so successfully I got a pain in my back, and had to sit up a little. At first, conversation was stilted. Mum and Dr. Tilbrook made small talk, and I chipped in a few comments too, but we all seemed to sip our drinks at the same moment, and this led to awkward silences. Finally, Dr. Tilbrook placed his cup (Mum's best, naturally) decisively down upon his saucer and began his pitch.

"I'm glad to come over to see you," he said. "As you know, I've been seeing Charlotte for six weeks now—"

Charlotte, I thought. No one calls her that unless they're Mum in a bad mood or someone who's never met her. He hasn't got very far.

"—and it is always useful to touch base with patients'

families once in a while. So I wanted to talk to you about how Charlotte is getting on, and see if my interpretation agrees with yours."

Mum nodded eagerly and clinked her cup down on the saucer a little too loudly. I finished my tea, balanced the cup on the sofa armrest with infinite care and folded my arms. Dr. Tilbrook coughed uncertainly. "Well," he said, "perhaps we should begin with your perceptions, Mrs. Fletcher. If I could ask you to—"

"Oh, of course." Mum was a little flustered, but she quickly composed herself and began carefully. "Well, I think we've seen a lot of improvement in the last week or two, haven't we, James? I think Charlotte has been much more content to take part in things. She's not shutting herself off in her room, moping from one end of the day to the next. She's a lot less irritable too."

Dr. Tilbrook was listening very closely, his head slightly tilted to one side. He didn't move a muscle, so appreciative was he. When Mum finished, he took a reflective sip of coffee, and nodded.

"I'm very pleased to hear that she is getting involved in the world again. But do you think, Mrs. Fletcher, that Charlotte is *inwardly* coping? Have you had a chance to talk to her about her lost friend, or how she is feeling now?"

Mum frowned a little and thought hard. I slumped lower in the sofa. "I've *tried,*" she said, "but it never does any good. In fact it sets things off on the wrong footing whenever I do. I'm afraid my daughter resents me if I try to come too close.

And I was advised, by the hospital, not to—you know—push her too much."

Dr. Tilbrook nodded in an understanding way. I fidgeted. Mum seemed to have nothing more to say.

"What about the nightmares, Mum?" I said. She seemed to have forgotten them.

"Oh. Yes. Well, James and I have heard Charlotte at night once or twice. She talks in her sleep, gets agitated—"

"Talks, Mum? She shouts! Screams sometimes too. She's having bad dreams, all the time."

"James's bedroom is directly through the wall. He hears things more than I do."

Dr. Tilbrook turned his attention to me. "Could you tell me anything more, James? These take place most nights, you say?"

"Yes. But she won't talk about them. I'm—we're—a bit worried about it."

"What do you think, doctor?" Mum said.

"*I* think it's important," I continued. "I really do. The dreams must be disturbing her, distracting her. But she never talks about them—she locks it all inside. I know she's doing more stuff now, during the day, but she's never interested in it. She's just going through the motions, Mum. Her mind's elsewhere."

I told them about the notebook I'd seen that morning. Mum frowned, but Dr. Tilbrook just smiled a little. "There's something about the night that's holding her attention," I continued. "That's what's weird. I mean, if I was having bad dreams, I'd be terrified to go to bed. But Charlie can't wait—she's always the first one upstairs."

I ran out of steam. Dr. Tilbrook levered himself back in his chair and flicked his hair into place with a jerk of his head. "Very interesting, James," he said. "Well, I can see that it is upsetting to witness these dreams, but the good news is that I don't think you should worry. Let me tell you why."

His fingertips came together and formed a little steepled arch in his lap. "In my opinion," he said slowly, "Charlotte is making good progress. Why do I think that? Firstly, for the reasons Mrs. Fletcher mentioned. She is getting on with life. When I talk to Charlotte, I find that she has not let grief overwhelm her. She is starting activities again such as the cycle rides she goes on with you, James. They mean a lot to her, though she may not be able to thank you for them now. And think about all the swimming she does—that's especially striking; think how healthy it is for her to *want* to return to the water. These are all good signs.

"But of course the grief is still inside her. It would be strange if it were not. So how does she respond? Well, it would be easy enough for her to shut it out, let it fester deep inside, but no—Charlotte is meeting it head on. That is what the nightmares are, James—memories of the tragedy, which Charlotte must wrestle with if she is to work it out of the system.

"It is very good news that she is writing about it. I gave her that notebook, James, and I've suggested she control her experiences by writing them down, so that she can talk to me about them when she wants to. It helps create objectivity, you see, if you try and record even upsetting things like nightmares. It is a vital part of the healing process. Every time she experiences a bad dream, and records it, she is working her way a little more into the understanding of loss. And gradually, as she learns to talk to me about what she sees and feels in those dreams, she will learn to control and come to terms with what has happened."

"I'm so glad," said Mum. "You see, James."

"What has she told you about the dreams so far?" I said. This was all very well, but it didn't seem to explain her secrecy, her odd detachment during the day.

"Not very much. I know they are very vivid, but I could not get her to give me any more details. They will be fragments, replays of the event, that sort of thing."

"So how do you know they're helping? I saw her. She's in real distress."

"Now, James—"

"Don't worry, Mrs. Fletcher," Dr. Tilbrook said soothingly, "James is quite right to be concerned. But although Charlotte hasn't talked to me about them yet, I fully expect her to do so soon. From a few little hints she has given me, I think she is about ready to confide in someone."

"I think we should look for her record," I said. "She's hidden it. I couldn't find it."

"Don't hunt for it," Dr. Tilbrook said. "Don't break her

trust. She'll show it to someone when she's ready." By his voice, I knew *someone* meant him. "She's working her way to a solution. We've just got to be patient. Thank you, Mrs. Fletcher, another half cup would be lovely."

I sloped off then, leaving them to chat about nothing. Mum had heard what she wanted to hear. I had heard nothing to reassure me. I went up to my room, passing Charlie's door as I went. It was half open, with an air of invitation and defiance. I looked at my watch. Charlie might be back in the next hour or so. That didn't give enough time for a thorough going over. *Don't break her trust,* Dr. Tilbrook had said. Well, he and Mum might be happy to let Charlie struggle along unaided, but I wasn't. It seemed to me that a bit of brotherly treachery was exactly what was required.

Fourteen

"Max . . . help me."

My head was in my hands, my hair spilling over my face. I was shivering with fear, sick with it. My heart lurched inside me as I waited for the rustle of dry fabric, the bony touch. Without thinking, I called his name.

"Max . . ."

"I beg your pardon?"

From behind me, a voice, quiet, enquiring. I raised my head a little and peered out through the cascade of hair. Across the grass, I could see the next row of trees in the distance. They were a long way off—there was no point in running.

"Do you need help?"

The voice seemed to come from very high up. Then I remembered that I was crouched on the ground. It was no good. I had to face it, whatever it was. Slowly, I drew one knee forward, then the other. Shakily, I got to my feet. Fine.

Now I was standing. But it was still behind me. And so, with little shuffles of the feet, I turned and looked.

And screamed.

Green eyes, like buried pebbles, gazing into mine.

A long thin face with pale green hair.

For a moment I was back in the swirling water, with cold thin hands clutching me, drawing me down. . . . I nearly fainted, but then my eyes registered the rest of what I saw.

It was a man's face, with eyebrows raised in mild enquiry. It was leathery lean and, though the bright eyes were flecked with green, I had been mistaken about the hair. It was tinted by the emerald light of the foliage above, but now I saw that it was brown—curly light brown hair that hung low to fringe his face.

He was tall, angular in body, and wore a pair of flannel trousers, brown shoes, a shirt, and colored waistcoat. And his head was slightly cocked on one side, as if he were waiting for something.

Fear still hung heavy in my stomach. What should I do? He was not attacking me, just standing there, with a quizzical expression. Should I speak? What should I say?

"Have I startled you?" the man said.

I cleared my throat, which was very dry. "Um, yes," I said. "I thought you were someone else."

One of the stranger's eyebrows climbed a little higher. "Indeed?" he said. His voice was soft, slightly amused. He seemed to be expecting something more.

"I've had a bit of a shock," I said. "Sorry I shouted."

"Not at all." He didn't seem threatening, but I had had more than enough. I wanted to get away, to be by myself again. I stepped forward as if to pass him.

"Which direction have you come from?" he said suddenly. His voice caught me by surprise, and I answered him.

"Through the forest."

"I know that." The stranger shifted impatiently from one long thin foot to another. "I mean beyond the trees. Which direction did you come from?"

This left me a little at a loss. "I don't know the exact direction, I'm afraid. There is a hill back there which I had to cross. And before that, a whole ridge of crags with desert beyond. I came over the desert."

The stranger's eyebrows shot up so far they almost disappeared under the looping curls of his forehead. "Really?" he murmured. "As far as that? I am impressed."

Despite myself, I was pleased by this reaction. "It's taken a good while," I added. The desert went on for days and days. But I crossed it all right."

"Very determined." The stranger scratched the side of his chin.

"Yes. And before that I crossed the sea." I was swelling up a bit at the evident magnitude of my achievement but, as I said this, the stranger laughed.

"Oh yes?" he said. "How did you do that then?"

And I had no idea, of course. I couldn't think back beyond the beach. I was silent. The stranger's eyes were on me, unblinking. Eventually, I knew I had to speak.

"I'm afraid I don't know," I said. "It's strange. I just woke up by the beach. It's all blank before that."

"Naturally," he said. "It would be odd if it were otherwise."

I suspected I was being made a fool of. "Well, I'm sorry I disturbed you," I went on. "I had better be going. Good-bye."

I began to move off, but the man had turned and was walking alongside. "Perhaps we are going the same way," he said.

This was unexpected. What should I do? He was the first person I had met (I would not count the dead thing), and though it made a change to talk to someone, I had no idea what he wanted. Every time his green eyes sparkled, the memory of the women in the water rose again into my mind. I wanted to be free of him.

"Are you looking for someone?" he said.

That shocked me. He could see in my face that it was so.

"How do you know?" I said feebly.

"Perhaps I have seen him."

I stopped right where I was. I didn't bother hiding my eagerness. "Tell me," I said. "Who have you seen?"

But the stranger held up a long thin hand. "Wait. We should do this properly. Introductions first, then information. I don't know anything about you."

"All right," I said. "What's your name, first?"

"Kit. Yours?"

"Charlie."

"Good. That's better. Well, Charlie, tell me who you are looking for, and I'll tell you who I've seen."

"I'm looking for my friend Max," I said. "He's about my age. A bit taller than me. Brown hair, straight. Bit podgy. White trainers. Jeans maybe. But I'm not sure what he's wearing actually."

To my surprise, the stranger—Kit—gave a sudden decisive nod. "I've seen him," he said. "He came through here. A couple of days ago."

"Two days!" The time gap wounded me even as I celebrated the confirmation. "How was he? What was he like? Did he speak to you?"

"I did not speak to him. You don't, when you meet walkers in the wood."

I felt a chill of unease. "What do you mean?"

"You haven't seen anyone else yourself?"

"Well . . . I saw *something.* Back there, just now. But it wasn't a person. It was . . ." I couldn't say it.

Kit seemed sympathetic. He patted my shoulder. "That must have been a shock for you. Especially if you saw one of them close up."

"You're not saying that Max is like . . ."

"No, no. Not at all. He seemed in the peak of health. But it is wise to be cautious in the forest. I only approached you because it seemed like you needed help. Besides, I could not have stopped Max even if I wanted to. He walked very fast."

"Excuse me, I must get on." Two days ahead of me, Max was alone among the terrible things of the forest. I began to stride forward, tears welling in my eyes, but Kit kept pace beside me.

"You seem distressed, Charlie," he said. "Perhaps I can help?"

"I must catch him, that's all." I was breathing fast, short of speech, panicking a little, not thinking straight. Above us, the great trees rose up to ever more gigantic heights, shrouding us with green stillness.

"Wait for a moment."

"Sorry. I must get on." Fast as I could. No time to pause.

"Wait."

Something in the tone of voice. A soft command that broke through the fraying tension and the clamoring anxiety in my head. Wait . . . I halted, eyes wide and staring. He walked a little way ahead of me, and looked upward.

We were standing at the foot of one of the giant trunks that supported the distant overarching roof. This trunk was so huge that as I craned my head right back so that my neck really hurt, and followed its column up into the dim reaches of the cathedral space, the straightness of the trunk was distorted and actually appeared to bend into the distance. There were one or two branches that protruded here and there along the giant trunk, and these were well supplied with thick green foliage. I thought that just one of these branches must be the size of an ordinary oak tree, but here they were tiny, dwarfed by the colossal trunk and the space beyond them. In the distance was the true canopy, an indistinct haze.

Kit gazed for a moment into this enormous space. There was not a sound in the forest. Then he spread his arms out wide.

It suddenly seemed to me that the distant canopy far overhead changed color, as if a shutter to the side had suddenly been opened to the sun and its bright light allowed to fall across the leaves. A dash of brilliant white flared across the emerald canopy, mingling with the green for a moment, seemingly about to be engulfed by it, and then, with a kind of surge, fighting itself free. It grew more and more defined as I watched, a lowering roof of flickering white and silvers, brightening as it fell.

For a minute it denied every attempt to make out details; I had to squint, my eyes hurt with the light. Then suddenly, everything came into focus, came into being—a hundred thousand glorious white birds with plumes and wings and tails of silver descending through the air.

Down and down they came, and now the air was rushing with the noise, the astounding, ear-convulsing quivering and sighing of a million feathers on the wing.

Down they came, and with the whole space filled with the hurtling mass of shimmering beaks and claws and with the noise drowning the air so that I feared even to breathe, I crouched myself into a ball and covered my head with my arms. Then the noise was on me with a great roar and a buffeting all around. My ears stung, I gritted my teeth with the pain of it. . . .

Then there was silence.

I opened my eyes and looked out from under my arm. I slowly stood. The forest floor was transformed as if by the coming of winter. In every direction it was a sea of white. A hundred thousand birds had alighted on the turf, blocking out the grass except in the space immediately around my feet. The great black columns of the trees erupted starkly from the whiteness, and a little way off, the stranger stood with his arms aloft, a single white bird perching on one hand.

All the birds were still. The stranger caught my eye. He smiled.

"The forest has many treasures," he said. "You must learn to watch for them. If you do, they will give themselves up to you. A fool has eyes only for the ground."

I said nothing. My eyes were too busy, drinking it in. For a few minutes neither of us moved. The birds remained on the forest floor, lifting their heads a little or pecking at the ground. It was as if a breeze were stirring a white sea. Suddenly my companion gave a slight twitch of his hand and the bird upon it lifted itself into the air. As if at a prearranged signal and with an explosion of sound, every other bird rose too, rendering me blind and deaf at their passing. Then the noise boomed and fell, and they were gone: a flickering layer of white, rising silently into the gloom.

"How did you do that . . . Kit?" I said at last. My mind was spinning with it.

"Practice. Anyway, I merely wanted to divert you. Are you calmer now?"

I nodded.

"Well, Charlie, perhaps you would like to tell me your story. How you came to be here. As I said before, I might be able to help you."

"All right, but I can't stay long," I said, a flicker of my old anxiety returning. But Kit sat himself beside a tree, signaled me to continue, and closed his eyes. Seeing him relaxing there made me want to rest too. So I sat myself down a little further off, crossed my legs, cleared my throat, and began.

Fifteen

Kit listened without interrupting once. It took a long while, for I had never tried to communicate the truth before, except in my diary. As I got into it, I found I was standing up again, walking about, gesturing, giving the story my all. When I had finished, Kit sat staring up at me impassively with a calm and reflective expression on his face. He wasn't in the least bit disturbed.

"Interesting," he said. "Not unknown, although a trifle unusual in the details."

"But I don't understand! I don't understand anything!" I found I was almost shouting. He was so matter-of-fact it infuriated me.

"What don't you understand?"

"Anything!" I did shout this time.

"Ask then," he said simply.

"All right." What question to ask? Start at the beginning. "Who were the women in the pool?"

Kit pursed his lips. "Hard to say precisely. I have never met anyone like them myself. But I can tell you this. Some entrances have guards, who watch and wait for those that seek entry. On this occasion, the wardens were happy to help your friend through. He was lucky."

Lucky? Strange, I had not thought of Max that way before. Yet it was certainly a most peaceful country, with more delights the further you went in. I thought of the wondrous birds. Perhaps luck *was* involved. "Are there many entrances?" I asked.

"There were once more gates than could be counted. You could find them in hawthorn or apple tree, in hard stone or yielding bog, in fleeting shadows on the edge of fields. You could often guess the times they would open too—at harsh noon hour when the shadows vanish or at midnight when the moon is full. Many people walked through them. Now there are fewer by far, most in inaccessible places—in mines and high crags, marshes, and wells. They close up and are forgotten. Few find them. I say again, your friend was lucky."

He had been looking up at the branches overhead as he spoke. Now he suddenly looked straight at me. "They are the true entrances," he said. "But they are not the only way in, as you well know. Dreams are entrances too. So it has always been and always will be. A great many people find their way here in their sleep and wander awhile through the forests."

"That thing I saw—is it a dreamer too?"

"No. It is a lost soul, neither of this place nor your own.

It is best not to talk about it. It is the dreamers that are important. Most appear only fleetingly and drift in circles, lost among the trees. They do not know what they are looking for, you see, and have no momentum, no direction. Very soon they wake and recall nothing. They rarely find their way back to the forest, and never to the same place."

"But I do," I said. "Every night I do, without trying."

He nodded, and gestured to my leg. "You have been touched," he said simply. I felt the blood pulsing under the healed skin of my calf, marking the place where the woman's fingers had clawed me. I shuddered at the memory, yet Kit was still talking.

"For those that have been touched, it is not so easy to forget," he said. "Memories of the forest linger during the day. You are drawn back here by those memories and by the determination of your own free will. Nevertheless, despite all that, you are still bound by the constraints of dreams." When I frowned, he said, "Put simply, you cannot stay here when you wake. The other world always draws you back. It is an unusual situation. Your access is both easy to achieve and impossible to maintain." He smiled ruefully. "How very tantalizing."

It was quite true. I arrived here with great ease, every night, bound to Max by my love for him. I followed him as quickly as I could; perhaps I even moved faster than him for the duration of my sleep. Yet it was all to no purpose. When I woke, Max drew further away from me again. At this thought, anger filled me.

"It's so unfair!" I shouted. I stamped my foot on the ground. "All I get is glimpses and never a chance to catch him." My friend nodded sympathetically.

"It is difficult," he said. "Travelers such as Max walk fast and don't look back."

"It's going to drive me mad," I said.

"Of course, there is one solution." Here Kit got to his feet. He put his hand on my shoulder.

"What?" There was something patronizing in his action. I expected the worst.

"You can give up the chase. It is only your bond to your friend that is bringing you back here. Reject that bond and you will not come back. Your friend will go and you will forget." He squeezed my shoulder gently.

So I was right—he was doing me down, trying to make me give up. What did he think I was going to do? Draw back and leave Max forever in this place?

"I'm sorry," I said politely, "but I couldn't live with myself if I did that."

Kit gave a little half smile. His fingers clenched warmly on my shoulder. This time, the squeeze was firm and lasting; it seemed the touch of equals.

"Lucky Max," he said, "to have a friend like you." He suddenly drew back and flung himself back down on the turf beside the path. He indicated the ground beside him. "Sit down then," he said. I sat.

Kit tucked his long legs up so that his knees almost touched his face. He folded his arms around them. "As I say, your problem is unusual. Most visitors don't remember their visits here, and most come only once or twice. You are exceptional. But then, you came very close to passing through the entrance yourself and its attraction for you is very great. And, if you don't care to take leave of Max . . ."

"I don't," I said.

"So what other options are open to you? Well . . ." He rested his chin on his knees and blew out a sigh of heavy thought. There was a long silence.

"Where is Max going?" I said, suddenly.

"You don't know?"

"I told you, I don't know anything about this place."

"My apologies. It's just that I've been here for such a long time, I forget. . . . Well, listen to the silence a moment."

I closed my eyes. We had been speaking in hushed tones, as befitted this great valley of sleeping trees. White birds perhaps flew far above our heads, among the distant eaves of the enormous space, but not a sound of them could be heard.

"For most of the year," Kit said, "the woods are silent. They are never empty, of course; they are filled with animals, birds, and flowers, and people too, such as myself who wander through them. Dreamers and new arrivals also flitter here and there restlessly. Most times of year, they drift, marveling at the delights around them, and you would probably have caught your friend quite quickly if you had come then.

"However, at this time of year, things change in the forest. The reason for this is the Great Fair."

Whether or not there was a suggestion of suppressed excitement in his voice, the very words made my heart quicken. *The Great Fair.* A frisson of anticipation ran down my back.

"This fair," Kit said, "is held by the people of this country to celebrate the turning of the seasons. It heralds the approach of winter." There was a bright green light shining in his eyes as he spoke. "And every imaginable delight and festivity takes place in it. For the most part, during the rest of the year, the people of this country are a solitary lot. We mind our own business, you might say. But during the time of the fair, all manner of games and entertainments occur. Just off the top of my head, at last year's fair, we had jugglers, dancers, acrobats, amusing burlesques, mimes and pantomimes, theatrical productions of every hue, fire breathers and stiltmen, carnivals and circuses. There were tumblers, tightrope walkers, rope climbers, and javelin riders. There were mystery plays and games of Spite, Jackdaw, and Curlicue. A lake was frozen over especially for ice sports, and a sloping hillside was carved into an amphitheater for the free enjoyment of all. Thousands attended, drawn as much by the delicious food on offer as for the entertainments themselves. Each year new recipes are devised solely for the duration of the fair, never to be eaten again. I myself tasted roasted chestnuts dipped in honey marinade, sweet acorn dumplings, hot marzipan pillars, and grebe fillets with lavender and ginger. While I tasted, my ears rang with a thousand merry sounds, from the trilling of pipes and the clamoring of horns to the booming of unattended drums. Choirs sing, traders cry, and all the folk of the fair raise such a hullabaloo that the trees for miles around vibrate in sympathy to it. It is a marvelous and most exotic fair."

"It sounds it," I said. His voice flooded me with sensations. My head was awhirl with images, with imagined scents and sounds. For a moment, all thought of Max went quite out of my head. Then he returned with a flurry of guilt and I tried to get myself back on track.

"Is Max going there, to the Great Fair?" I asked. I hoped so.

"Certainly. All those who have come into this world like Max through real and proper entrances"—in other words not through dreams, like me—"will now be making their way to the site of the fair. From all around it they congregate. If you could look down on the forest like a bird from high above, you would see hundreds of figures like Max all moving toward the center, as if they were on invisible spokes of a wheel. They are all answering the call that goes out, summoning them to the fair."

"What call is this?" I hadn't heard anything.

"You haven't heard it because you are not truly of this country. You are only half here, after all. The summons is picked up by us all living here, but it holds a particular compulsion for wanderers like Max."

Far, far above, a flock of birds, maybe twenty or thirty strong, drifted like a white wisp of twisting paper against the vaulted ceiling of the canopy. "The centerpiece of the fair," my friend continued, "is the Great Dance, when all newcomers to our country are celebrated and welcomed. It takes place on the last night of the revels. Max will be traveling as fast as he is able to take his appointed place. By joining the dance, he will become one of us, a true inhabitant of this country."

"And if he doesn't?"

"He will have to wander anew until the next dance takes place, neither eating nor sleeping, nor laying down to rest. Truly, he will be hurrying there at the best speed he can muster."

"Perhaps I can meet him at the fair."

"Perhaps, but I should warn you of one more thing. Once he has joined the dance, Max will truly be of this country. He will forget you and his past life. Then he will not know you if he meets you among the stalls and side shows of the fair."

At this, a great grief welled up inside me. "How then can I catch him?" I said. "It is hopeless."

"Perhaps, perhaps not. There are ways. I will tell you when we meet next."

"Meet next? Tell me now! I can't waste time."

"You are waking. Can you not feel it?"

And I did feel it, deep down inside me. A shifting of my body, a lightening of limb, a sudden subtle sense of dislocation, so that the very movements I was making—the sharp turns of my head, the urgent gesticulations—seemed unconnected with my brain. Cause and effect were breaking apart. I tried to get up from where I sat but my body no longer obeyed me. I began to lift out away from myself and the scenery of the great forest flickered and grew dimmer as if lit by a guttering candle.

All of a sudden I left that place. My friend grew faint and his shape vanished, although even as I felt my sheets and pillow grow hard and definite against my body, I heard his voice ring out a final time.

"Do not worry. I shall be waiting," it said.

Sixteen

James suspects something, I know he does. He was hanging around me all day, trying to get me to do things with him. He was watching me all the time, driving me mad. When I told him to get lost he got quite funny with me and refused to go, and in the end I had to shout for Mum to come up and order him out of my room. Even then he wouldn't leave off—he's just knocked on the door again, asking me to watch a film with him downstairs. I didn't bothering answering of course. I have to sleep.

I was trying to keep myself occupied by writing, while waiting for drowsiness to kick in. I didn't really need to, of course: I now remembered without effort everything that happened to me in the forest. Kit's every word rang in my head, clear as clear. The same wasn't true for the tedious day at home. I could hardly concentrate on it and forgot what people told me as soon as they said it. It just wasn't important.

As he promised, my new friend was still there when I returned to the cathedral of trees. He was sitting motionless beneath the mottled shadow of one great tree pillar, head bowed slightly, eyes two glinting specks in the dimness of the forest.

"Time has passed," he said to me in greeting. "A whole day and more."

"I know. It took me ages to get to sleep."

"More time is lost." He didn't need to say this. I had been worrying about it all day. I almost thought he was rubbing it in, but his voice had a sad and heavy tone.

"I know. So tell me—I mean, you said you were going to tell me another way to catch up with Max, before he gets to the fair." I couldn't help sounding a bit wheedling. More than at any time, I felt helpless in this wood, in the race with Max.

"Did I? Well, yes, there are ways. But they aren't easy. Perhaps—"

"I'll try them. Whatever they are. Please, tell me."

"Let me ask you a question first. How do you spend your time when you are not here?"

"During the day? Don't know, really. I forget. Mooch around a lot. Go out. I don't see friends much any more. Maybe my brother, sometimes, but he's a drag."

"And how do you feel about this time? Do you enjoy it?"

"What do you mean, 'enjoy it'? You're getting to sound like Tilbrook. No, I don't, not at all. Because—"

"Yes—because what?" He leaned forward eagerly, as if confident of my answer.

"Because I'm not here of course, and because Max—"

"—is getting farther away all the time you sit there, doing nothing, listening to fools prattle around you without understanding the urgency you feel. Yes, I know what you're going through, my dear, and it isn't pleasant at all. Isolation stings, doesn't it? But don't worry. You don't have to let them grind you down. The way forward is right under your nose, if only you can see it. But that involves getting off your backside and looking, during the day."

He paused for breath, and I paused to absorb the flurry of words that had bombarded me. I hadn't heard him so impassioned before and all his shots rang true.

"Go on," I said at last.

"I will make myself clear." He flexed his fingers a little and rolled his shoulders as if preparing for great physical exercise. Then, with a bound, he leaped to his feet, and began to pace the turf in front of me, six steps to the left, then to the right, wheeling round tightly in between.

"Charlie, you will never catch up with your friend here," he began. "I explained that yesterday. You are not fully in this country and in your absences Max moves on. What you need are ways to speed up your movement through the forest, to jump forward, if you like, along Max's trail."

He made another turn and continued. "The other

danger you have is that the farther behind Max you are, the less easy it is to follow him. The trail goes cold. In which direction do you think he is?"

I opened my mouth to speak, and found, to my horror, that I could not answer. All this time I had been cast-iron sure of my direction, straight and confident as an arrow. And suddenly, I no longer knew. Panic rose in my gullet and I began to sweat, while all about me the forest seemed to close in, silent, watchful, endless.

The other waited for a moment, then seeing that my answer would not come, resumed his pacing. "You see," he said, "it becomes more difficult. Nor would it help to make straight for the fair. Its location is very tricky to find; often it seems to shift, even during the duration of the Fair itself. I do not know where it will be this year, and you will certainly not find out, unless you are drawn there by the scent of your good friend Max."

I said nothing. My position seemed worse with every sentence he uttered.

"But what you must realize," he went on in a slightly lighter tone, "is that there are more ways into this country than the one Max found, more ways in than just through dreams. Also, you must understand that while Max is walking through the forest, heading for the fair, he is still close, on one level, to his old country, to the places he once knew."

"What, do you mean his old home?" I asked. "Or the places we used to go? I've not felt him there." I was thinking of the steel factory's emptiness, its desolation.

"You haven't looked hard enough. You haven't listened out for him, for the echo of the footsteps or the sound of his voice. I'm not saying it's easy work, far from it. Max is distant; he's in the forest, walking. But he is also close to these sites that he once loved, and if you look hard enough, you may find ways through, shortcuts if you like, that will leap you on through the forest, closer to him. Think about your journey so far. Your going is slow now. Has it always been so?"

I thought back, and almost as if it were in a dream of another life I recalled the first faltering steps on the beach, then on the dune, then the desert, leaps onward each one with gaps between them. "No," I said slowly. "To start with, I traveled fast. Before the desert, I was a little farther in each time."

"And tell me, was there anywhere you visited, at that time, that Max and you both knew?"

"Only the—only the mill pool, itself. I visited that again, right at the start."

"Exactly. You were close to Max then, very close, and closing with each dream. Since then, you've lost the trail during the daytime and that has meant you've lagged behind at night." He stopped pacing suddenly and looked me hard in the eye.

"You need to search by day," he said. "Search for places where Max is close."

"But where?" I was flummoxed by this new suggestion. I had written Max out of my daytime life so entirely in the last few weeks that I could hardly begin to think.

"I can't tell you. You know him better than anyone, don't you? That's what you told me. So you must remember the places where Max was happiest, where he was most—" He broke off, turned to face the vastness of the forest. "You must think hard. It's up to you."

It *was* hard to think, standing there in the forest, with the greenness muffling the drab memories of my home and town. My friend seemed to realize this. He smiled and turned to me from his contemplation of the cavernous spaces.

"Don't worry now. It may be easier when you are there."

"Okay." I shrugged. "But I don't understand what this will achieve. If I go somewhere that Max is . . . close to. What then?"

"It will draw you closer to him here in the forest. Your experiences will change, will quicken. And if you're lucky, you will find yourself catching him well before the dance occurs. Perhaps, you will even find another entrance . . . for yourself."

He finished, but I was hardly listening any more. One thought was resounding through my head. *Find yourself catching him.* Yes, and then . . . And then what? What happens when I do? I simply had no idea. But remembering his silhouette in the distant glade, I felt it would at least be enough to touch him and make him turn to me.

All of a sudden, I noticed that the light in the forest was changing swiftly, growing perceptibly darker. There were distant flutterings and calls from the lower branches of the great trees and the air became close and warm. The upper reaches of the distant canopy turned from emerald to sullen olive green and the rows of trees stretching away on all sides began to shorten as the darkness closed in.

"A storm is coming," Kit said. He loosened his collar. I felt damp under the arms. A bird flew low across the space in front of us, silently and fast, making for hidden shelter.

"I have to go," Kit said. "I have stayed here too long, talking with you."

"You're going?" For some reason the thought of his absence shocked me. The forest pressed in all around. Even in the growing warmth, my hands were cold.

"I must. Perhaps we will meet again. I will keep my eyes open—for your friend, for you, and for anything else that might help you."

He shook my hand. I was too bemused to speak. Then he turned and was striding off noiselessly through the dark grass, with the olive shadows patterning his thin, high shoulders and his long hair. In a few moments, he was a dull smudge in the encroaching dark, silhouetted between the pillars of two trees. Then he was gone.

I was alone in the forest and I did not know which way to go. All at once I heard a roaring in the heavens as unseen rain began to crash against the topmost leaves of the canopy far overhead. But I had stood there for many heartbeats shadowed in the warm darkness of the wood before the first raindrop struck the grass beside my feet.

Seventeen

When it happened, I was under Charlie's bed, trying not to sneeze. I had a theory that she might have hidden the notebook somewhere in the mess of girls' magazines strewn in the grimy underworld beneath her bed. I knew my way around there a bit—some of those mags had girls' problem pages that repaid a bit of reading—but I hadn't bargained on all the boxes of old toys and teds and games I'd given her, and above all all that dust. So I was rooting about, snuffling like a pig, when the doorbell went and I was still only halfway out when Mum opened the door and the trouble began.

First of all, I just heard an alien voice, a man's, raised in anger. For half a second I thought it might be Dad, but even as I thought it, I knew I didn't recognize the voice. Or did I? Maybe it did ring a bell. I wriggled my way out from under the bed and rested a moment with my head on the floor, listening. Mum was trying to say something, raising her voice too, but she kept being shouted down. I still couldn't hear properly, so I got up, kicked an incriminating doll's box back out of view, and crept on to the landing.

The man's voice came echoing up the stairwell. Mum had evidently failed to get him into the lounge, which was always her first objective with any visitor.

"Do you think we have to put up with that?" he shouted. "Do you? It's bad enough that we have to be in the same town as you without her come lurking round our house! What does she want? What *can* she want?"

"Really, I'm sure she can't have intended—" Mum's voice was taut with agitation. She was very upset. I started for the stairs.

"Can't she? With me at work for the first time today—and to come back finding my wife weeping in the hall!"

I froze on the second step down. All of a sudden, I knew who he was, this man whose voice had rung a bell. I knew where I'd heard it before, just a few weeks earlier, giving the reading in a silent church with that same voice breaking as he fluffed his lines. That was it. That was when I'd seen him. At his son's funeral.

You know sometimes you realize something so nasty or awful is happening that the sweat breaks out on your hands and your back and neck go cold all at once? This was exactly what happened to me here and I was rigid. I didn't know what to do. Like a coward I waited in the shadow of the stairs, waiting while the terrible voice went on, quieter now.

"I'm relying on you to find out what she wants. It's your

responsibility. I'm not blaming the poor girl, but . . . you'd think we'd just be allowed to get on with our lives. My poor wife . . . That's all. Just tell her to leave us alone!"

The door was slowly closed. I was frozen on the stairs. I heard Mum go back into the lounge. I followed her. She was sitting on the arm of one chair, holding her head in her hands, and I went over and put my arm round her.

"It's all right, Mum," I said. "It's all right."

She gazed at the wall. Her face looked creased and old. "I don't think it is, Jamie," she said.

"What was she doing?" I asked quietly.

"That poor woman. Charlie was around their house. She was seen from the upstairs window. She was down there, in the alley behind, creeping in the yard. Sitting there, walking around. That poor woman. She went down to talk to her and she was gone. But later she saw her again, at the front, by the gate. Not doing anything. Just standing there, she said, as if she were waiting. Can you imagine, Jamie? What can they think of us, to let her do a thing like that?"

I hugged Mum tight. It was the first time I'd done that since Charlie had come back from hospital. She needed that hug badly and I needed it too.

"Don't worry, Mum," I said. "I'm sure there's a simple explanation. She's working things out for herself. We'll have a word with her when she comes home." I sounded confident, but even as I said it, I knew that I didn't have the faintest idea what to do or say.

I had been right to be skeptical of Dr. Tilbrook's glib

diagnosis. Far from confiding in him, Charlie was more wrapped up in herself than ever. She was dozy and vague, like she was drugged or something. It was hard to get any sense out of her.

Heavily I climbed the stairs again. That bloody notebook. More than ever I felt it was vital to find out what it said. Perhaps it gave some clue to what she thought she was doing. But for that I had to find the thing—and she'd hidden it too well. She'd not had it when she'd cycled off. It was in that bedroom for sure. But where?

Eighteen

Kit told me to look for Max in his old haunts, places he used to know and love. I don't really understand how, but Max is still close to these places, even though he is in the forest too. If I go there I might find myself closer to him, or another way to get through.

<u>Possible places</u>
The steelworks
Max's house
The canal

There are more, but it's so hard to remember. Anyway, that's enough for starters.

It was the obvious place to try. Max's house, I mean. I hadn't been back there, even to his street, since the morning of the mill pool. To tell you the truth, I hadn't wanted to go anywhere near it because I was fearful of how heavy his absence would feel there. I thought it would be the steelworks, only worse. But now, all of a sudden, that made it a place of opportunity, not loss. So I cycled over without hesitation, hid my bike in the alley and stepped over to his back gate.

Max's mum and dad both work, so I knew the place would be empty. The gate was locked, but Max had taught me how to open it by standing on a brick and craning my arm over the top. It was stiff, but I worked it loose. I pushed the gate open, just far enough to slip inside, and shut it again.

It was the same old yard, with all the piles of bricks and cinderblocks Max's dad had bought years ago for the extension to the kitchen he never built. But the grass had grown up long around them and the flower bed, which Max's mum had once kept moderately sane, was choked with weeds, unkempt, unloved. And all Max's rubbish—the rusty swing, the collection of soft footballs, the various bats and guns and broken games that used to litter the place—all that old clutter had been removed.

That would have bothered me before, but now I was concentrating on my search. I had half a mind to try the back door and see if they'd left it unlocked. Maybe I could creep up to his room, look for him there. But then Max had never been too keen on staying indoors. This yard was our old HQ, where we used to plan things. It was best I stay here.

But what should I actually do? Now that I thought about it, Kit had given me no specific instructions. There was no point *looking* for Max in the ordinary way. Different measures were called for. I sat on the cinder blocks and closed my eyes, trying to be receptive, calling to him in my head. I tried to remember what we had done here, the spy games, the assault course, the raids on the opposite yard . . . Quite a bit came back. It was fun. Max would enjoy remembering it too if he was nearby. What about the water fights and the time we tried to climb on to the kitchen roof to retrieve a tennis ball? Come on, Max? Can you hear it? Are you near?

I opened my eyes suddenly, aware of a little sound up at the house. I was just in time to see a pale face pressing against the net curtains before it moved back and disappeared. Max's mum. A shock ran through me, half fear, half annoyance. She should have been at work, not loitering at home. Now she'd ruin everything. She'd be coming down to interrogate me: What was I doing? Why was I here when Max had gone?

I didn't want any of that, so I slipped out through the gate again, shut it, ran down to my bike, and was off up the alley before she could have opened her back door. Around the corner I stopped for a rest. Now what? I couldn't go back, for a bit at any rate. I didn't want to try anywhere else either. So I drifted along on aimlessly for a while, up this road and down that, and suddenly found myself, almost by accident, around the *front* of Max's house. I stopped pedaling and stood there, one foot on the pavement, looking up at Max's bedroom. Something was wrong with it—and I couldn't tell what it was at first. Then I realized that his old curtains, the ones with the rockets, had been taken down. That made me feel bad. What would Max be thinking? What else might they have done to his room? Were they trying to forget him? I craned my head to try to see in, look at the wallpaper, get a view of his old cupboard. Where was that stack of games? It looked like they were gone too.

Then, like a bad dream, that same pale face appeared from nowhere at the window, looking down at me. She was there again! Guarding the place, preventing my access! I could see her mouthing something. A fist banged against the glass. I looked away in disgust. Just ignore her. I could do nothing for the moment, so I cycled off up the street.

I spent most of the rest of the day down by the canal in the cold, eating crisps and reading comics from the newsstand. I was in a bad mood, and didn't want to go home. It infuriated me that Max's own parents were frustrating my attempts to find him. There was almost no chance that Max would be drawn back to his house if they were ridding themselves of all his things, all his own memories. It was hopeless. Evening drew in and I was still there, hunched on a wall overlooking the towpath.

At last I got cold and stiff and forced myself to move. I decided to head home though, I wasn't looking forward to returning to the forest now that I was lost. Something made me take the long route back, past Max's house. I kept away from the front and wheeled the bike back up the alley to a patch of shadow under the wall opposite the gate. I stood there looking at the house. It was dark except for a light on in the kitchen and one in the upstairs toilet window.

I remembered that window. It overlooked the roof of the kitchen. It was possible, if you were small and sinewy, to climb on to the inside window ledge, carefully avoiding the bottles of shampoo and deodorant stacked there, and then squeeze yourself headfirst through the window. Then, if you wriggled forward like a snake and carefully gripped the outer ledge in both hands, you could twist your feet out and down onto the flat kitchen roof. Max and I both did this several times when his mum was out. Then came the time when Max got too fat and got stuck halfway, with his stomach protruding from one side of the window and his bum from the other. And like a fool I had gone first, so I was trapped on the rooftop together with a packet of biscuits we'd filched from his mum's pantry. And no matter how hard I pushed or pulled, I couldn't shift him one inch, and we'd had to wait until his mum got home and came into the loo and got the shock of her life, seeing her son's fat bum hanging through the window. She'd used butter to get him out, and he was sore round his sides for days.

And then, suddenly, as I was thinking of this, of all the embarrassment I'd felt, and how funny we'd both found it afterward, I found myself standing among trees in a part of the forest I didn't know, leaning against a trunk and laughing. There was a cool breeze against my forehead.

The trees were smaller here, more like ones in an English wood, and I could hear animals moving among the bushes around me.

Then I became aware of a particular noise, a gentle, hesitant rustling, very slow and deliberate; the sound of bark being touched by a moving hand. And I knew that it came from the other side of the very tree against which I was leaning. I kept quite still, doing my best to think of that ridiculous scene: the window, Max's legs kicking behind the glass, the sound of shampoo bottles careering into the bath. And the dry rustling, rasping sound continued round the side of the tree, closer and closer, until I even thought to hear the crush of grass under someone's foot.

Closer, closer. The other sounds in the forest had died away. The trailing hand must be very near. Perhaps, out of the side of my eye, if I just turned . . .

"You!" Out of the forest, between the trees ahead of me, a dark lumbering form came running, arms raised, breaking the branches, tearing the trees in two, shredding the whole forest into strips which dissolved before me, to leave me staring once again with newly opened eyes at the darkening house, and Max's dad hurtling out of his gate right for me.

In a blind panic I grabbed my handlebars, fell onto the saddle and lurched forward, feet flailing for the pedals. Max's dad reached out, my foot made contact with a pedal, and with a single desperate push I swerved away to the side of his halfhearted clasp, almost up against the brick wall. I fended this off, scraping my elbow in the process, and then I was off, head down and sprinting along the dark alley. As I went, I heard him calling after me.

"I've spoken to your mother! She'll be waiting for you when you get home! And don't think you'll come back here! I'll get you if you do!"

I hardly heard him. I was too furious with my disappointment and my fresh new loss.

Nineteen

I haven't written much for a few days. It's all been too depressing. I'm lost in the wood, wandering, no longer on the trail. I see birds, and some animals at a distance, but no people. The animals are deer, I think, though it's hard to be sure. Once, I thought I heard a cry somewhere far off, or maybe it was a horn. I don't know. I haven't gone back to Max's house and nowhere else has helped yet. The canal and steelworks gave me nothing. I don't think I'm in the right mood. Mum and James are acting oddly. Mum's not going out very much and she's made me stay in to watch videos. Why can't they just leave me alone? I'm feeling very low. There's no point even writing this, except I'm so bored.

Try as I might to put a good spin on it, I knew I had messed it up down at Max's. I should have gone over when his mum and dad were asleep. And I knew now I'd have no luck if I went back. Max wouldn't be there any more.

I was quite down and my journey through the forest made me worse. I was getting nowhere, the dreams dragged on and on and sometimes I didn't even bother to walk, I was so dispirited. I would sit glumly under a tree, watching the birds. I had come to a part of the wood where the trees were smaller, more personal and scrubby, and there was activity all around. I started seeing squirrels in the branches above and colored birds with long feathered tails. They all frisked about in quite a lively way, but I was so low, I hardly cared.

Then one day I had my big chance. I had summoned up the energy to walk and was swiping irritably with a stick at any ferns I passed. All of a sudden, I was disturbed by the sound of loud crashing from the forest on my right. I was circling the margin of a great steep hill and the noise was coming from the thick brushwood that clogged the area. It drew nearer and nearer, and I fell back a little and held my stick out unconvincingly in front of me.

The crashing reached a crescendo—then out onto the path spilled Kit, covered in prickles and burrs and all out of breath. As soon as I recovered from my shock, I greeted him warmly.

"Very glad I found you," he said at last as his gasping drew more measured. "Saw you from the top of the hill and came running. Something you'll be interested in."

It took another few minutes for him to get his breath back fully, while I was forced to wait, beside myself with impatience. Finally, he sat himself on the bank beneath the thicket, brushed a few prominent twigs from the front of his jacket and took a good look at me from under a lowered brow.

"Pardon me for saying so," he said, "but you don't seem to be in the best of shape. Not as I remembered you, anyway. Not the energy or determination you once had . . ."

"Nor the direction," I said. "I'm lost. I've been trying to follow your advice, but I've had no luck so far." I told him my account, and he shook his head ruefully.

"You were unlucky," he said. "It was the right thing to do. But listen, you may have no need of that advice any more. I have news."

He paused a little, milking my growing excitement. "On the brow of this very hill I have found something which may be of use."

"What have you found?"

"A certain tree." Here he picked a large thorn from the belly of his waistcoat with finger and thumb.

"Go on! What, is it tall—a lookout place?"

"No." He suddenly signaled me to him, taking a swift, furtive look left and right as if someone might be near. I drew close.

"This tree," he said, "is very rare. It is in most respects unremarkable. Not tall nor great of girth. Its leaves are a drab puce green.

"However, this tree bears fruit, and this is where its one unusual quality resides. These fruits are unattractive. They are small and wizened and their skin bears a passing resemblance to that of a wrinkly old crone. However, they are very good to eat—very sweet they are, very sweet indeed." Here he licked his lips and smiled.

"But even that is not the central fact about these fruit," he continued. "It is not the taste of them—but what the taste can do! Just one mouthful of this fruit and your greatest desire will be your command."

I frowned. "They grant wishes?"

"Not wishes. *Desire*. The most heartfelt thing you crave, that you lust for with every ounce of your being. This is not some fairy-tale lamp to rub to give you tin-pot wealth or fleeting fame. You do not have to speak your wish or even think it. It comes to you, unasked for, from deep inside. It is there, in the fruit, waiting for you if you want to taste it. Only, you must be confident of what you desire, for it obeys even those cravings you have not yet acknowledged to yourself, ones that you perhaps ignore or even fear. It might catch you by surprise."

"I know very well what my one desire is," I said. "That is why I am here."

"Exactly. This could be a shortcut to your friend. How it will work, I don't know; it can never be predicted. But if you do want to try, I will lead you to the tree."

We began the climb through the thicket of gorse and scrub, which, though seemingly impenetrable from the path, soon opened out a little to allow us fair headway. Even so, I was scratched all over through my clothes by the treacherous thorns and spikes that seemed to protrude at every level. Kit led the way, appearing to recall perfectly each twist and turn of the route, though the hill was a monotonous waste of low-lying bushes in every direction.

After a while, we broke out above the level of the trees around us and once again I received a high view of the endless wood. The sky was darkening toward evening, and the light was noticeably poor. My friend looked about him and then pointed.

"There," he said.

I followed his gaze. A little way off, rising slightly above the brown-green scrub, was a single solitary tree, warped and stunted by the winds of years. It was a sorry sight, with too few twisted branches, each one sporadically spotted with leaves. Here and there among them were tiny flecks of bright green.

We approached. So scrawny was the tree that its topmost branches were only a little higher than my friend's head, and its knotted trunk would have been thin enough for me to ring it with both hands.

"Here it is then," Kit said. "All you need to do is eat one single fruit."

He indicated a particularly contorted fruit hanging low, just at eye level. It was near enough for me to reach out and pluck it. The skin was a rich, mottled green, flushed with color; it was a very ripe fruit. It seemed to be hanging on to the branch by the weakest of threads.

"Tell me again," I said, "about how it works. What does it do?" I realized suddenly that I did not understand at all.

Kit's head leaned forward a little in a very earnest

manner. "All I can tell you is that it will make things a lot easier for you. Think about what we have talked about, think about the difficulty of your quest. You are having to conduct two searches at once, in two different worlds. And though you are determined and skillful, it is tiring you. You are already weary. Who knows if you will find your friend before he reaches the fair? Nothing is certain. You are badly in need of aid. This fruit may be that help."

"All very well," I said, "but I still do not really understand this fruit. You say it grants desire. Tell me, how do you know such things?"

He straightened suddenly to his full height, and smiled broadly. I took a step back—I had forgotten just how tall he was. "Simple," he said, "I know because I have tasted the fruit myself."

There was a far-off light in his eye; for a moment he did not see me; he was gazing inward at a remembered pleasure.

"Your desire was granted?"

"Oh yes." What it was he did not tell me and I did not like to ask. But I could see how powerfully the memory affected him. At length he roused himself from his reverie and turned to me again.

"So, Charlie," he said. "Taste it. You have nothing to lose." He reached out and plucked the nearest fruit. The broken stem wept a single tear of sap and was still. A sweet fragrance, heady as the scents of early summer, drifted in the air as he handed me the fruit in silence. I held it in my hand. Ugly though it was with its soft, overripe and blotchy skin, I thought it the most delicious-looking food I had ever seen. Its perfume made my head reel with pleasure.

"Eat," he said. "You will go to join Max."

The scent was all around me, tingling against my skin. I felt a sudden upsurge of delight and eagerness. The pressure of my love for Max crushed me, and I suddenly felt that he was very near. I could scarcely breathe with the anticipation. I could not take my eyes away from the hideous, delightful fruit in my hand.

One bite was all that was needed. Max was just moments away.

As I drew the fruit to my lips, I could see my friend smiling.

Twenty

I don't know when I actually became aware of the noise coming from Charlie's room. I had drifted out of sleep and had lain half-conscious in the warm darkness for many minutes before my brain logged in to the soft, slow thudding noise sounding through the wall. Reluctantly, I opened an eye. The bedside clock showed 2:13; the room was pitch black, and *thud, thud, thud* went the muffled rhythm through the wall.

This noise unnerved me. Normally it takes ages for me to wake up properly, but now I found myself sitting up rapidly and cocking my head to listen. *Thud, thud, thud.* So soft was it that I could barely catch it through the natural hissing of my ears.

I got up and padded out. Down the landing in two steps to Charlie's door. It was ajar. I looked in. The orange light from the alley flooded the room, giving it an unhealthy radiance. I saw at once that Charlie was asleep. She lay on her back with the sheets thrown off, and the orange glow reflecting with a stippled sheen off her mangy old pajamas. Both her hands were clenched into fists. Her right arm was twisted up against her chest, her fingers wrenching at her pajama top. The left arm was outstretched, so that the fist brushed up against her bedside cabinet. It was this fist which made the noise as, every few seconds, when Charlie gave a little shudder or jerk, it banged softly against the wood. Then I noticed her feet too. The toes were clenched.

Whether it was a nightmare or a fit, I didn't like the look of it at all. I stepped into the room and slowly approached the bed. Then I got close enough to see Charlie's face and I grew really scared.

Even in the sickly orange light, I could see that she was deathly pale. Beads of sweat were studded across her brow and rivulets of tears ran down the side of her face into the pillow. Her face was rigid with fear or pain, but her eyes flicked back and forth under the lids and her lips moved; she was mumbling something. I bent close, listening.

". . . what does it do? . . . I do not understand this fruit . . ." Snatches of words, fragments only, meaningless. It was only a dream, but even as I looked I thought to see her complexion worsen, as if the color that remained were being sucked out of her with a straw.

For a moment I was frozen with indecision. Should I leave her to sleep? No—whatever the nightmare was, it was affecting her so badly she was becoming ill before my eyes. She began to shake, with violent shudders like the worst kind of flu or fever, and her color was still draining away. I wasted no more time.

"Charlie! Come on, wake up!" I shook her gently by the shoulder. The fabric was drenched with sweat. "Charlie!"

No response, but a frown flickered across her forehead. I shook again, harder. The frown deepened, she half opened one eye, then closed it again.

"Charlie! Wake up!"

Then something horrible happened. She let out a low lingering cry—half snarl, half scream. The hairs rose on the back of my neck. I stepped back, loosening my grip on her shoulder. What had I done? Was it dangerous to wake someone from a feverish sleep? For a moment more I watched my sister, my heart thudding against my chest. At first she seemed asleep still, but then, all at once, both eyes opened wide and she looked at me, vacantly, uncomprehending. As she did so, the tortured lines began to fade away across her face.

"Charlie? It's me, James."

"Whuh?" Her voice was very faint.

"It's James. Are you okay?"

"The fruit—"

"You were having a nightmare, Charls. I had to wake you." The light was coming back into her eyes, and she began to focus on me for the first time.

"A nightmare . . . ?"

"Yeah, you were tossing and turning, looking really bad. I had to wake you. What were you dreaming?"

Her brow furrowed; she trawled her memory. Suddenly, a light dawned there. She remembered it, whatever it was.

"Oh, James, you bloody fool!"

"Charls—"

"What the hell did you do that for? I was about to eat . . . Oh, you've ruined it! You've ruined it! I might never get another chance!" She struck out wildly with her fists, missed me by a mile, then writhed around on the bed like she'd gone mad. I stood there dumbstruck. Finally, she buried her face in her pillow and clenched it around her head.

"What are you going on about, Charls? It was only a nightmare."

She flung the pillow to one side and beat her fist against the bed. "A nightmare? It was the best thing that could have happened and you've completely messed it up!"

"What?" This was stupid—I knew what I'd seen. I did my best to remain calm. "Listen, you were getting sick right before my eyes. You were pale, you were crying, thrashing about. It was like you were fading away. Believe me, I did the right thing to wake you."

"You had no right to wake me!" She was sitting up in bed now, shouting. "I might never get back to him! I had agreed to taste it—"

I knew she was still half asleep but, even so, my temper began to get the better of me.

"Don't give me that! You don't know what you looked like—you were really bad, really sick. Don't think I'd go around waking you up for fun! What was this dream that was so good that it makes you mad at me?"

"Don't lie!" She ignored my question. "I'm not ill, I'm fine."

"Maybe now." And I had to admit that her color was a good deal better than before. But that wasn't the point. "You're fine *now*—thanks to me!"

"I'll never forgive you for this, James! Never!"

So that was the outcome of my good deed. I shouted back a little more, for form's sake, but to be honest my heart just wasn't in it. Charlie was apoplectic, working herself up into a rage that I just couldn't match. It was completely over the top. From her standpoint, I'd just interrupted a dream—that was all. From my side, well—I knew what I'd seen. Or did I? It was all becoming a little unreal. By the time Mum surfaced, drawn by our shouting as a shark is drawn to blood in the water, I wanted nothing more than to go as far away as possible and leave Charlie to dream whatever she pleased.

Of course, as soon as Mum put her head round the door, we both stopped, neither of us wanting the laborious task of filling her in on the other one's injustice. I quickly sloped off to my room. What Charlie did, and whether she went back to her precious dreams or not, I didn't know—and didn't care.

Twenty-One

James has ruined it. Completely ruined it. If I'd had one moment more, I'd have been back with Max, I'm sure of it. But James woke me up. And now Kit has gone, and has probably given up on me completely. When I got back, I wasn't on the hill anymore, but back down in the forest, and though I've tried to two nights running to find the tree again, I can't. Another chance has gone, wasted.

I'm not speaking to James anymore.

I have given up looking in the forest. I'll never reach the fair. All I can do is go on searching the places we used to know.

<u>Other possible places</u>
New Park
Quarry
Skateboard rink

In fact, I came close again, sooner than expected when I wasn't even trying. It was around lunchtime. Mum had been annoying me more than usual with talk of getting me back to school. I'd missed half the term already and Dr. Tilbrook thought I should rejoin the class next week.

I didn't want to, of course. It would get in the way of my search. I suppose Max and I did spend a lot of time there, but we never did anything much together during school hours and I sure as hell knew Max wouldn't be hanging about there now. But I could hardly say why I didn't want to go back, and with Mum pestering me to know what I felt, I felt obliged to reassure her. So school was booked in for a week's time. Mum was very pleased, and to celebrate suggested fish-and-chips. I volunteered to fetch them if only to get out of the house for a while.

Luigi's Golden Fry is a couple of blocks away, over the road on the corner opposite the video store. I've been going there for years, off and on, and Big Luigi knows me pretty well. He knew Max too, of course, and what had happened, and when I stepped in to his shop, he put down his big chip fryer, came around the front of the counter and gave me a big greasy hug before I could stop him. He's all right, though, is Luigi. He didn't actually say anything, just went back around the counter and tossed the chips.

"All right, Luigi," I said.

"It's good to see you," Luigi said. "One big cod? Lots of vinegar?"

"Two. Just one with vinegar, please. The other one's for Mum."

"Okay. You want curry sauce?"

"No thanks. No, all right, Luigi, I will on my one."

Max used to smother his fish with curry. And mint sauce. That's why he was getting so fat. I didn't like it so much myself, but it seemed the right move that lunchtime. I dawdled in the shop while the new batch of chips was bubbling, looking at the faded luncheon-voucher stickers on the glass. Luigi gave me a bag of batter bits to munch. Finally he wrapped Mum's fish up, lashed mine with sauce and handed it to me, open in the paper.

"How much?"

"Go on. On the house."

"No, come on, I can't take this. Mum'd kill me."

"Go on, get out. It's good to see you."

"Well, you too, Luigi. And cheers—thanks a lot."

I left the shop, holding Mum's parcel under my arm while attempting to pull some of the new chips out from under the smothering of sauce. I turned the corner and walked along, dipping the chips, tasting the sauce. It was very good. Then someone called my name.

I looked up. A couple of people were in sight: a woman with a shopping bag and a young, grungy bloke with gray jeans. I didn't know either of them and they weren't looking at me. I looked behind—two men in the distance, heading for Luigi's, and a young woman with a pram on the other side of the road. For a long moment I stood still on the pavement, with a chip drooping foolishly in my fingers. A car passed me, going fast, and turned the corner with screeching wheels. Then silence.

I was mistaken, must've been. I ate the chip, walked on.

"Charlie!"

Now this time I knew I'd heard it. And I thought I knew the voice too.

I looked about me wildly. There was no sign of anything, just slabs of building, brick and road, with people moving slowly along under the leaden sky. No sign of anything. Then the voice came again. I spun around, scattering an arc of chips on the pavement. Where from? It was curiously distant, but I felt I could almost sense its direction.

"Char—"

Two cars came along the road, dawdling along with revs too high, drowning the sound, spoiling my concentration. Shut up! Hurry up! They slowed for the corner, turned and were gone from sight. Their drone faded with agonizing slowness. Silence grew again. I stood there, straining to hear.

There! Across the road, from down that alley . . . Quick—

Five seconds later, I was looking down between the houses. An ordinary alley. No one there. An old car, propped on bricks, halfway along. A line of washing suspended between garages. That was all.

No, listen!—there it was again! A voice calling me from down the alley, past the car. Where was he? Now I was running, feet plashing hard on the cobbles, nearly twisting over in the ruts. I left a trail of chips behind me. What remained of my fish was held tightly in one hand. Mum's cod swung wildly in its bag from my other arm.

Down the road, past the car, under the washing. Stop a moment. Listen. I could hear the blood beating in my ears. Nothing more. A pink sheet waved feebly in the breeze behind my head. I smelled its cleanness, and then the warm curry wafting from the mess of fish and paper in my hand.

"Charlie—"

Farther on, down the alley. That was where it came from. It was nearer now, nearer and louder. And it was his voice, I knew it. I ran on, down behind the sleeping houses, past the open doors of sheds and garages, my footsteps echoing back at me from wall and gate. Down I ran, toward the end of the alley and the open road.

"Charlie . . ." Could I hear a note of desperation in that call? Was it dying down, trailing off? Whether or not, it gave me wings: a final burst of energy carried me forward, faster than ever. It came again once more, softly now, but very near, round the corner at the end, just out of sight.

A last few pounding steps with hurting shins, and round the corner, two strides forward, straight out into the road—

Then a rush of movement, a screeching noise, a blast of air that battered me, and a bag of cod and chips flying up and outward in a lazy curve to collide and shatter in a thousand fragments against the hood of a moving car.

Twenty-Two

Max called me today, and I answered him. And I would have seen him too if the bloody car hadn't nearly knocked me down. I had to run for it, there and then, before the woman could get out and catch me. Worse than that, I lost the chips, and had to lie to Mum that Luigi's was closed.

But it didn't matter when I got back to the forest, because I found myself in a different area. I'd made a jump forward, which meant I must be closing in on Max somehow. I strode onward with renewed energy. This part of the forest is full of pine trees, dark and silent. The layering of needles on the floor is very deep here; around some trunks, it's drifted up like snow. Once I tripped and my arm disappeared into the needles up to my shoulder, like it had been swallowed. I trod carefully the rest of the way.

Twice I heard horns ahead of me, and once I think I heard voices too. Perhaps I'm nearing the forest's edge?

* * *

In five days time I was due to go back to school and I was determined to find Max before I was cloistered away again. I hadn't long, but my experiences at Max's house and Luigi's had given me new heart. And there were plenty of other places where we had gone together if only I could decide between them. Which would Max choose? Where would he be waiting?

The next day was irritatingly taken up with Mum things, mainly shopping. She insisted I go with her, and it was mainly food shopping at the superstore out of town that made it even more unbearable. James looked especially smug when he learned of our expedition and went off to school happy. We'd not spoken since he cocked things up.

It was on the way back that we passed the scrapyard. Mum had followed the railway to get to the ring road, and on the way back I caught sight of the tall wire fence surrounding the scrap-car graveyard. This massive waste lot runs for about half a mile alongside the railway line and it is filled to the brim with rusting cars. They're stacked four or five tall in places, and sometimes they even crush them down a bit to make them even easier to fit. There's a giant crushing machine near the entrance that they used to run sometimes during the week though I'd not seen it in operation for years. It had a huge steel plate on a pile-driver arm, which used to flatten the car into oblivion. All in all it was a brilliant place, and Max and I got in twice to climb the stacks. It was extra dangerous because of the watchman.

Seeing it as we drove past put it right into the forefront of my mind and, once there, I couldn't get it out. As soon as we'd unpacked and put the food away, I was all for heading off, but then Mum scuppered me completely.

"You're not going anywhere, Charlotte. We're going out to Greg's for dinner and no arguing. Go and wash, then watch TV or something. When James gets back, we'll go out straight away."

I didn't bother arguing. Mum had grown a bit tougher in the last few weeks, and I can't bear her shouting like I used to. So that put paid to my immediate plans. We went out dutifully and I'm pleased to say James enjoyed it just as much as I did.

When we got back, I went up to bed and waited for the others to get to sleep. It didn't take long because everyone was worn out with the restraint of being polite to Graham. When Mum's light had been off for half an hour, I slipped down the stairs and out the front. I didn't take the bike in case anyone heard the scraping in the shed.

It took twenty minutes to reach the scrapyard, longer than I had expected. The night was cold too and I was feeling it through my jacket, even though I'd run most of the way. The road was completely empty and the pinkish streetlamps along the edge of the fence illuminated tidy spotlit circles of wire and concrete, leaving the rest of the street quite black. I stood in front of the high wooden double front gates of Bullock's Scrapyard and looked at the mass of chains fixing the gates and the razor wire running along the top of the fence. Bullock didn't like visitors.

Northern Plains Public Library
Ault Colorado

I shivered. The wind had picked up and I was chilled. Max and I had found a hole in the fence, but I couldn't remember where it was. It would probably have been fixed long since. I should have brought Dad's old wire cutters from the shed. What was I playing at, coming unprepared? I trotted along the fence for a while, looking in at the dark irregular mass of car stacks, their blackness broken near the streetlamps into spotlit columns of battered metal. I would need a torch too if I wanted to get around in there.

No point hanging around; I would have to come back tomorrow. Then, as I turned in the road to begin my slow way home, I felt a sudden certainty within me that Max was very close indeed. Beyond the wire, out of reach for the present—but very near. Tomorrow I would find him. Tomorrow it would have to be.

I ran most of the way home, went to bed, lay down, and was soon in the forest.

As I walked, I found the way becoming more and more difficult. There seemed to be no end to the pinewood; on the contrary, the grim straight trunks grew closer and closer together with every few steps. The duff underfoot was softer and deeper and more treacherous than the night before, so that every step forward was slow and cumbersome. I regularly had to support myself by leaning against the trunks and the bark proved flaky and weak under my hands.

To make matters worse, the lowest branches—all sharp, dead, lifeless sticks—grew ever closer to the ground, so that I had to duck my head as I progressed. And the light was very poor. The thick black upper branches of the pine trees blocked out the sun, which was weakening toward evening. Only the presence of a strange green-white mold on the trunks of many of the trees, which gave out a dim luminescence, enabled me to feel my way.

I had been advancing uncertainly for some time in this fashion when I suddenly stopped dead. For no apparent reason—there had been neither sound nor movement up ahead—I suddenly felt myself in danger. I could feel the hackles on the back of my neck rising.

There was utter silence in the forest. I had seen no birds or animals all that day. I waited ankle-deep in pine needles, with eyes wide and the mold light gleaming.

Then the sounds came, little pitterings and patterings like the fall of rain. Softly and swiftly from the greeny blackness up ahead, growing in sound and number all the time. And still I saw nothing.

I pressed my back against the nearest tree. Great flakes of moldy bark fell away and lay glowing dimly at my feet. The pitter-pattering sounded all around me now in the shadows among the trees, and I heard a snuffling. Then the sounds cut out.

A dry dead branch projected from the tree beside my head. It had a sharp tip. Without turning my head, I raised a shaking hand and tugged. It snapped off with a crack that stabbed the silence. Trembling, I held it out in front of me like a sword.

A minute passed. I did not move. I did not blink.

There was a snarling in the darkness straight ahead of me. Something edged out into the half-light from under the black branches. A long, low shape, slinking close to the ground, red eyes fixed on me, mouth open, teeth bared.

I was pressing backward so violently on the tree that the bark drove its pattern through my clothes and into the flesh of my back. I whimpered, the branch slipped in my sweaty palm.

Then, with a rush and a roar, the wolf leaped at me. I caught a glimpse of the gaping jaw, the yellowed teeth, a blur of blackness enlarging to swallow up the wood. I raised my stick and, as I did so, my right foot lost its balance in the duff. I slipped to the side, fell; the stick swung upward. There was a confusion of wolf, stick, and tree; all three colliding as I hit the ground directly below. I felt the rasp of claw, a shrill thinness of pain, a hot scent, a heavy thud, and a shower of bark and blood. Then, all in an instant, the wolf had fallen on to me—half covering my legs—and had risen to its feet, wheeled about where it stood and was gone into the night with a guttural moaning, and blood flashed darkly on my broken stick.

All around in the dark circle of the pinewood, a great howling rose up.

This woke me from my stupor and set me unsteadily on my feet again, ignoring the pain that lashed my arm and the panic that turned my guts into liquid. I ran from the tree, away into the forest, each stumbling step sending an impact spray of needles all around.

A swift black shape erupted from the trees to my right, leaped at my side. I slashed out with the stick. The wolf wheeled in midair and, yelping, half fell against the nearest trunk. I ran on as the howling burst out anew behind me.

For a while I had a clear path among the pines. I found a narrow depression, perhaps the bed of a dried-up stream, which wound its way between the trees. Here the needle cover was less deep and it was low enough too to let me run at speed, avoiding even the lowest trailing branches. But the light was fading and the depression was inky with deep shadow. Once I missed the place where it turned sharply, and ran right up against a tree, grazing my palm and the side of my face.

Close behind came a dust storm of needles, stirred up by running claws.

Now the streambed petered out in a morass of blackness. I missed my footing, fell against a steep bank, began to struggle up it. An eager snarling came from around the corner I had just passed. Frantically, I climbed, slipping on the dry needleskin, fingers hooking into the damp layers beneath. All the time my stick was lodged between the thumb and finger of my right hand. Low-slung whip-thin branches slashed my face, I smelled the mold on the earth. I got to the top of the bank, launched myself forward, ran two steps more and the ground disappeared beneath me. I was falling, head over heels, over and over, a gathering snowball of needles rolling down a slope. My stick was dislodged, my hand gave it up, it fell away. I could do nothing except tumble, arms and legs flailing, over and over . . .

. . . and then I hit a tree, driving the air from my lungs and sending me scudding to a stop in a newly plowed drift.

I opened my eyes. I was lying on my back under a blanket of needles. There was a break in the trees above me. The red light from the dying sun pierced the place where I lay. I tried to lift my head, pain stabbing in my neck and arms. Slowly, slowly, I raised myself on to my elbows, and looked back up the slope.

And the wolf sprang straight at my face.

Twenty-Three

Try as I might, I couldn't ignore Charlie completely, and that night she forced me right back to my old anxiety. I'd woken up around four and was heading for the loo, keeping one eye closed to try to convince my brain I was still asleep. When I came out on to the landing, I noticed the light shining through the slightly open doorway of Charlie's room. What was more, there was the faintest sound of music too, as if someone was listening to headphones.

I paused on the landing. I had a choice: pee or peek. Well, there was no contest—at four in the morning my bladder beats curiosity every time. But when I finally emerged once more, her light was still on and the music still played. I sidled to the door and looked in, blinking at the brightness.

Charlie was in bed, white as a sheet. I could tell she'd been crying too. She was sitting bolt upright, reading a book and listening to her Walkman. There was an open notebook resting on her cabinet. Even at this distance I could see it was half scrawled with her spidery writing.

I was tempted to leave her to it; if she wanted to stay up all night she was welcome. She'd been snubbing me completely since the time I'd woken her and I'd given up in disgust trying to be nice. But I could tell she was upset now. She wasn't even reading properly, just gazing past the page at nothing, eyes boring into the bedclothes. No, I was probably asking for it, but . . .

I knocked very quietly. Charlie didn't notice. So I pushed open the door a little. The instant I did, she jumped like she'd been electrocuted, terror etched on her face. That's sisterly affection for you. I put my head fully around the door.

"Charls, it's only me. You okay?"

Her shoulders relaxed; she breathed out with a gasp of relief. Weird. I stepped inside and closed the door to. Charlie pushed her headphones back.

"What do you want?"

"You look terrified. Who did you think I was?"

"Nobody. Why are you awake?"

She was sullen and grumpy, but I'm an old hand at gauging my sister's mood and I could tell she wasn't unhappy to see me. That was something. I went and sat on the bed and clicked the off switch on the Walkman.

"You all right, Charlie? What are you doing up at this hour? I've got an excuse. I needed a pee."

"You're always needing one in the night."

"That's not true. Anyway, girls have to go much more often than boys. Smaller bladders."

"Rubbish we do."

"So what are you doing up? You should get some sleep. You look like you need it. Hey—what's that?"

She'd turned to face her bedside light and I'd suddenly noticed a mark on the side of her face. A graze, a bad one too.

"Where's that come from? That wasn't there this evening."

She was looking down at the duvet, not at me. I felt annoyed, pressed her for an answer. "Well?"

"I had a bad dream. Must've scratched myself." Now that *was* unusual—admitting it, and after last time too. It didn't exactly explain the graze though.

"What, you did that? Come on." I was working up to skeptical-brother mode, but then I stopped short. Charlie was looking really small and frail. I felt I should hug her or something, so I patted her feet halfheartedly through the covers.

"Yeah. And this." She took her right hand out from under the cover. It was wrapped in a hankie, but there was a spot of blood showing through it.

"What the hell . . ." I grabbed her wrist and unwound the hankie. She had a massive new cut right down the back of her hand. "Bloody hell, Charlie. You're not telling me you did this in your sleep."

She was. She started getting defensive too, so I didn't

push it. She wanted to talk a bit, for the first time in God knows how long, and that was enough. I tried to listen instead of lecturing.

"It was a bad dream. I didn't want to go back to sleep for a bit."

"Can you tell me about it?"

"No. Well, you'll think it's stupid. I was chased by wolves."

"Oh. A wolf dream. I used to have those when I was really little. I remember one where the wolf was waiting for me in the bathroom when I went—"

"Don't!" Oops. "It wasn't any old wolf dream. It was awful." She shuddered. "They were chasing me, and I tried to get away, but I couldn't. And at the end, one of them—"

She closed her eyes. "It leaped at me. And I woke up."

"Just in time. Did you know that you never quite d—come to a nasty end in dreams? You always wake up just in time. I used to have one when I was at the top of a ladder, falling forward into space. I went whistling down, with my stomach rising up inside to the roof of my mouth, and I was about to hit the ground . . . then—bang! I was awake. Nightmare. Oh—sorry."

My anecdotes weren't having the desired effect. Charlie looked like she was about to cry. "It's not like that with me," she said.

"Look, you've woken up. You're okay. Give or take the odd scratch." I could say what I liked, but those grazes were weird. "Listen, Charls. Nothing bad will really happen with a bad dream. It freaks you out, sure, but then you wake up and you're okay. You don't always have bad dreams, do you?"

"No. But I always dream."

"Yeah, but they're not all bad, are they? Chances are you'll be fine if you go back to sleep."

"No I won't. I'll be back with the wolves. And they'll kill me."

"Charlie, dreams don't work like that."

"Mine do."

"Oh well—" I wasn't getting anywhere with this. "Look, you try and get to sleep and I'll stay with you for a bit. I'm not tired now anyway."

"I'm not either. I'll be okay for tonight. Go back to bed if you want."

"Don't worry. Look, do you want to play a game or something? There's Ludo under your bed."

"How do you remember that? No, I'll be okay. Go to bed, J. I'll read. It's almost five and you've got to go to school."

This was true. And I had a test. "Well, if you're sure . . . You'll be back at school next week. Are you looking forward to it?"

"Yeah, I suppose so."

"Well . . ." We were running out of things to say. I was too tired to come up with much more now. Bed beckoned.

"All right. But listen, if you have any more bad dreams, come and see me."

"I'm not sleeping any more tonight."

"Please yourself. But remember what I said. See you tomorrow then."

"Yeah. Thanks for coming in."

"That's okay."

I went back to bed, and slept fitfully, dreaming about Charlie and her bleeding hand and face. When the clock finally went at seven and I stumbled out into the light, I looked into her room again. And she was still there, sitting bolt upright among her sea of pillows, plugged into her earphones, looking at nothing.

Twenty-Four

5:30 A.M.: I mustn't sleep.

James can't do anything. The wolves have got me. I felt their breath on me as I woke. They'll be there waiting when I next go back. They'll kill me the instant I sleep. I don't know what to do. Maybe they were there to stop me catching Max. Maybe I was getting close. . . . But it hardly matters now—I can't escape.

7:00 A.M.: I've made it to morning though I'm dead tired. And now I know what I have to do. It's the car scrapyard. It has to be. They're trying to get me before I reach Max. If I can find him at the yard today, before I sleep again, maybe I can get past the wolves, get to a new place, like Kit said.

If I don't, I'll fall asleep tonight and die.

That day was a bad one. It went sickeningly slowly. James went to school, Mum went out to work. I was tired all over;

there was nothing I wanted more than to curl up on the sofa and steal an hour or so's kip. But I couldn't—if I didn't want to die. What was more, I was aching all over from the fall on the slope. I'd really bashed my neck and it was stiff and painful to move. Worse than that and the cut on my hand was the gash where the first wolf's claw had ripped my side. It wasn't very deep, but I didn't like the look of it at all, even when I'd treated it with Savlon. It stung like mad under my top. But I was still glad James hadn't seen it, or there'd have been hell to pay.

Of course I cycled down to Bullock's yard straightaway to see if I could get in. But there was too much going on: men in tow trucks bringing cars, big lorries pulling out with stacks of wheels, fenders, hubcaps, windscreens. Even the big car crusher was in operation for half the morning, slamming the life out of corroded old wrecks, leaving the flattened shells to be hoisted up onto the stacks by crane.

I loitered around the gates and wandered around the perimeter of the fence, looking for the hole Max and I had made. I found where it had been, right on the far corner away from the gates, up by the bushes shielding the railway. Someone had filled it in with barbed wire, but it was a bit of a slovenly attempt and I thought I might shift it with the wire cutters and Mum's oven gloves. The other option would be climbing the fence. That was possible; it was made of looped wire and the loops were big enough to fit my shoes in, but the top was smothered in razor wire. On balance, the hole had it. My inspection ended suddenly when one of the men passing in a lorry shouted at me to clear off. I obeyed.

After that I went home and got my kit together: gloves, cutters, flashlight. Then, since I didn't have anything to do until the evening, I mooched around our area of town on the bike. There wasn't much going on, so I made for the New Park, which is on the opposite side of the town to the canal and railway. This whole area used to be filled with slag heaps and quarries filled with poisoned water: the by-products of the steelworks that were dotted round our town. A few years ago they began turning most of the valley that side into parkland, bulldozing the slag heaps into the quarries, draining the poison out and covering the whole lot with new earth. Then they sculpted a series of lakes and streams, added a few plantations, wood-chip pathways, and a tacky cafeteria with columns by the entrance. It's all very dull, but it is green, I suppose. Max and I were more interested in the workings they'd left up on the hill beyond the park. We'd get ice creams at the caf, then climb up to the quarry edge and chuck stones into the water.

At the entrance to New Park, a couple of grumpy workmen were busy erecting a stall. There was a sign up on the railings:

NEW PARK FÊTE

This Saturday and Sunday.
Games, Stalls, Tombola
Win a Panda!

I assumed the panda in question was a toy one, but you never knew. Whatever, the idea of a fête made me feel sick. It reminded me of the Great Fair in the forest, which Max might already have found, and of the dance, which he might already have joined. And here I was, grubbing about in a cheesy park with nothing to do except wait until dark, and feeling like death but unable to sleep. . . .

Town parks always depress me. I cycled off home.

Evening came eventually. I had tea with Mum and James and they talked a lot. Mum was off on a secretarial course in the morning. She probably felt guilty that she'd be away for the day because she suggested a cinema trip after tea. I refused; I was tired. James backed me up on that one. I wished I could have talked a bit more to him about what was happening because I was really scared about what the night would bring. What if nothing happened? What if Max didn't come? I couldn't make my brain work to think it all through.

The trickiest bit came now. I went to my room early and put off the light. I wanted to lead by example, encourage them to get to bed. It worked well enough. James soon turned in and Mum followed around ten to watch the TV in her room. I waited in the darkness, fully clothed under the duvet. I'd give them an hour, then get going.

It was a dangerous time. Sleepiness swamped my bones, pulling me down against the mattress, spinning my mind in lazy circles. I felt a terrible temptation to forget the plan, to let go and drift away . . .

. . . into the mouths of wolves. I forced my eyes open, furiously drummed my fingers against the bed, beating out the seconds. Time passed. Mum's light went off. My fingers went on drumming.

At last it was time. I got out of bed and reached for my rucksack, which held my essential kit. I didn't make yesterday's mistake. Plenty of layers to keep out the November chill. Now, through my door and down the stairs, keeping a wary eye on James's darkened room. Keys from the table, out the back, bike all ready, back gate open. Out and away, down the alley in record time. Away to the yard.

It was another cold one, with a nearly full moon peering out from behind a few livid clouds. There were still a few cars on the roads, so I rode on the pavements without bothering to switch my lights on. The street by Bullock's yard was empty as usual, the hulking columns of dead cars standing out starkly against the moon. I rode right around to the corner nearest the railway. What time? Twelve. Maybe one more train coming, otherwise I would be left alone.

At the fence I drew the wire cutters out of my pack. I put the oven gloves on and felt up and down the wire loops till I found the edge of the barbed wire. I didn't use my torch. That was for emergencies: there was always the night watchman to consider. Clumsily, I set about cutting. I couldn't see exactly what I was doing, but I tried to slice as many wires as I could around the edge of the old hole. The fragments of barbs played havoc with Mum's gloves, but I didn't care. The cutters were doing their job and the wire was falling away. Max would be proud of me.

In about five minutes I had disposed of the barbed wire and extended the hole a little into the bargain. The gloves and cutters went back in the pack and I took a last look round. No one was in sight. Then I was through the fence and into the yard.

When I stood up straight I had the immediate sense that Max was somewhere near. It was curious; I didn't hear him this time, or see him, but his presence was very close. A slight breeze blew from behind me, setting the long grass rippling at my feet. The nearest stack of cars was a meter or so away. It was almost entirely in shadow, but the crushed and gaping side windows of each car made the stack seem like a pile of giant skulls. There was a gap, the width of a man, between this and the next heap. I edged toward it, trying to recall exactly what Max and I had done when we had come here over a year ago. We had been trying to get to the car crusher at the other end, daring each other alternately to pass each stack. In the end we hadn't made it: the watchman had been prowling and we'd sped silently back to the hole.

It seemed enough to me now that I work my way deep into the yard. I could feel Max somewhere ahead. He would be waiting for me where he chose, calling the shots as usual. All I had to do was follow. Carefully, I edged forward through the gap and as I did so the moon came out fully from behind a cloud and illuminated the scene with a silver flood. I was in a narrow canyon of metal, twice my height and more in places, with the upper reaches lit by light and the bowels where I was walking plunged into shadow. The tops of the stacks shone as if they had been polished, while the moonlight rippled ceaselessly on their ruptured, corrugated flanks, making the contours fluctuate as I moved.

I kept a watchful eye out for Max. He was here somewhere—maybe playing with me, teasing me like he used to, waiting to jump out at me from behind a bumper or perched ready to leap from the top of a wobbling column.

The canyon came to an end at a large saloon car that was propped almost vertically against the side of one of the stacks. It had a colossal dent in its roof, which held the shadow and looked like a wound. Both the side passages ahead were pitch black. I fumbled in my rucksack for the flashlight and held it at the ready. Which way to go?

"Max!" I whispered it under my breath. "Call me!"

No answer came, but a cloud covered the moon. The canyon tops were lost from sight. I could barely see the hand in front of my face. I switched the torch on, angled it to the ground, and took the corridor on the right.

This passage met another, at a crossroads beside a vast pile of tires. There was a strong smell of petrol here. I turned to the left, keeping myself parallel to the railway, and headed on. Once I thought I could hear a whispering up ahead, but when I hastened forward it had gone.

Then I came to another intersection. I glanced to the right, then to the left—and, just as I turned, saw out of the corner of my eye something move far off between the stacks. A rapidly moving smudge of white that disappeared behind a pillar.

"Max!" Still I didn't dare raise my voice. I set off down the new canyon without bothering to listen for an answer. In seconds I was at the junction where I judged I'd seen the shape. I looked down the side passage. Not a thing—but surely, there was the whispering again, up ahead. I felt his presence all around me now, stronger than before, encouraging me to come.

I went down the side passage, fast as I could, my flashlight wheeling and swooping on the sheer walls on either side.

"Max!" I called out a little louder; I was too excited to bear the silence now. "Max!"

And then I saw it. Far off along the passage between the stacks, a long, low shape, a movement coming fast among the shadows. I couldn't make it out properly, not yet, but I stopped dead, right where I was. The beam of my flashlight couldn't reach the shape, but there was a pool of moonlight halfway along, at a point where one of the stacks had toppled. And into this spotlight came the wolf.

I had turned and was running before my mind had even framed the word. My rucksack was bouncing on my back, my torch was crazily sweeping light up and down as my frantic arms pumped the air. I knew I had no chance, I knew I would be caught, but I ran anyway because I didn't want to die.

And behind me ran the wolf.

At the end of the passage, I ducked to the left, and almost immediately saw the hood of a car sticking out at waist height from the nearest pile. I vaulted onto it, and grasping the empty window casing of the car two layers above, began to clamber up the rusty metal wall. My scrabbling trainers were only about seven feet off the ground when the wolf turned the corner and launched itself upward. Its teeth snapped together inches below me and it fell back to the ground. Gasping for breath, moaning with fear, I swung my feet up farther, using anything I could as rungs: window sockets, door handles, rust holes. Even as the wolf leaped up on to the hood of the lowest car and jumped again, I was five cars higher up, pulling myself up onto the flattened roof at the top of the stack.

I lay on the car roof, panting. Below me, the wolf set up a furious snapping and yelping. I could hear it pacing about, circling the foot of the stack, pawing at the ground. My mind was awhirl, I felt giddy with confusion and terror. The wolf had broken through, it had pursued me from the forest to the town. Nowhere was safe. And as I lay wide-eyed in the moonlight, sprawled flat upon the night-cold metal, for a moment it seemed to me that I was lying instead on a narrow pillar of rock, wedged tightly in on every side by pines.

The vision vanished, but the whining and slavering of the wolf still drifted up from below. Suddenly, it let off such a clamoring that the echoes erupted from the stacks, rebounding endlessly so that my head rang. I pushed myself up into a kneeling position and surveyed the tops of the stacks. They were all lit with moonlight, a silvery maze of narrow highroads split by coal-black canyons. If I could work my way along the tops, perhaps I could yet escape.

Gingerly, I got to my feet. To my great relief, the stack was rock solid. Rather to my surprise I realized I still had my flashlight in one hand. I stuffed it into my rucksack—both hands had to be free.

There was no time to be lost. Perhaps more wolves would come. Fortunately for me, my stack was part of a great connecting ridge of cars and I had a choice of direction. I chose the way that led toward the distant perimeter fence.

For a moment or two, my progress confused the beast, and I could hear that I was leaving it behind. But soon the sounds I made as I stumbled along from one roof to the next—scuffling, banging, tripping, half falling—alerted it to my position and it began to run along the base of the ridge, howling with frustration.

At first I did well, halving the distance to the far fence in a minute's journey. Then my luck began to run out. The long ridge of stacks came to an end; a narrow gap separated it from the beginning of the next. I didn't hesitate, but ran as fast as I could at the gap—and leaped. I soared over the gulf and landed heavily on the roof of the car opposite with a clang that set echoes resounding. To my horror, the whole stack swayed.

No time to lose. The wolf was keeping pace. I got to my feet and carried on but almost immediately found myself confronted with another gap, bigger this time. My heart failed me. I couldn't do it. I was six cars up, and the distant ground was invisible in a well of darkness below. It was simply too far to jump.

Then I saw the stack of tires. They were over to my right, a little nearer than the cars and, what was more, they extended in a shapeless heap right up to the edge of the perimeter fence. They were piled so high they nearly topped the razor wire. If I could make it there . . .

I retraced my steps to give the maximum run-up and tightened the straps on my rucksack. A frenzied howling came from below. Glancing down, I could see the mad eyes of the wolf staring up at me, reflecting the moon. I turned back, fixed my eyes on the tires ahead and ran.

Seven steps to the lip of the rock. My right foot met the very edge as it pushed. Into the void, arms out, legs forward, outlines of trees flashing past on either side, moonlight showering me as I fell through the air. Onto the tires with an impact that made me cry out. My fingers clutched for safety, my feet kicked out for a hold, as the tires I was on began to slide back down the steep scree slope toward the cliff edge. I launched myself upward, kicking a single tire backward out into the air. It fell into the darkness, and I had the satisfaction of hearing a loud yelping from below.

Now I was up at the top of the tire mountain. The fence with its sheath of razor wire was right ahead. I had no time to get the gloves. Trusting to luck I leaned forward, arching my arms and torso over the vicious spirals of wire, and grasped the topmost loops of the fence below. Then I swung myself out into thin air. I came down hard against the fence, grasping the loops for dear life with wildly swinging feet. It was easy, like vaulting a five-bar gate, and Max had taught me that long ago.

Now I climbed down, fast as I could. I hit the grass and ran for my bike, hearing the wolf howling and fearing at any moment that it might burst out of the fence after me. But though the beast ran alongside, once or twice snapping at me through the loops, it could do no harm. A maze of cars separated it from the hole. For the moment it was trapped.

In a few seconds more I had reached my bike and was off along the road, zigzagging under the streetlights. I never cycled so hard. Cold air whipped my face. And all the while I listened for the sound of wolves behind me.

So they had broken through. They were after me. Nowhere was safe. In a few seconds the adrenaline that had carried me out of the yard faded into nothing and I began to ache with fear. What could I do? Where could I go? Not content with waiting in the forest, now they had followed me here.

Unless they had followed Max. He was here too, somewhere near. I would have found him at the yard if they had not been guarding him so closely. But I was lucky to have escaped with my life.

I must not sleep, but I could barely keep awake. In a dream,

I made my way home, left the bike out in the yard, locked the door behind me, and climbed the stairs to my room. I shut myself in and switched off the light and sat myself in the shadows at the edge of the window, looking down into the empty alleyway.

In a few moments more I knew they would come.

Twenty-Five

Charlie was standing by my bedside. She had shaken me awake.

"Wha-smatter?" My eyes couldn't focus. Neither could my tongue.

"Get out of bed. They're here. I need help."

"Whadyoumean?" I remembered vaguely that I had told her to wake me if she needed me. Okay, don't get angry. "Whasup?"

"The wolves. They're outside. I saw them in the street. They're coming for me. Come on, James, get out of bed!"

For heaven's sake . . . Very slowly, I twisted my legs over the edge of the bed and struggled into a sitting position. "Don't worry. It was a nightmare. There's nothing to worry about."

"It wasn't a nightmare. I haven't been asleep."

"What? Charlie, it's five thirty! You're not telling me—"

"Hurry up, James! They're in the yard. They might get in."

"You know what it is, you're hallucinating from lack of sleep. You're really telling me you haven't been— All right, don't get mad. Wolves, are there? Okay, whereabouts? Go ahead and show me. And don't fret, I'll look after you."

"I saw them from my window." Right, it was time to get this over with as quickly as possible. It was Saturday morning and I wanted my lie-in. I brushed past her, noticing as my eyes cleared that she was still dressed, and went into her room. It's at the back of the house, looking down onto the yard. I looked out. It was still quite black, except for a couple of bathroom lights on across the way. Charlie's light was off and I was soon able to make out some of the details of the yard. Her bike slung across the center of the concrete, Dad's old shed, the washing line, the water tub, the back gate . . .

"Well, the gate's open, but there's nothing else to worry about," I said. Charlie had come alongside me, peeping out from the edge of the curtain. "No wolves out there."

"They must be in the alley."

"They're not. Look, I can see right along both ways. There's nothing there. You've been seeing things, Charls, which is no small wonder if you've been up all night. What's stopping you from sleeping? The wolf dreams?"

"They broke through and chased me tonight. Nearly got me too."

"Where did they chase you? You've been in bed."

"No, I went out."

"You went out? Where to?" I was quickly realizing that wherever Charlie was coming from, it was way, way beyond me. I just didn't know what to say. All the sensible stuff I was trying to come up with made no impression: she just pulled the rug out from under my feet every time.

"Down to the car yard. I was looking for—there!" Her cry was so sharp and sudden that I flinched back from her. "Look!"

"Where? For Christ's sake, don't do that."

"By the gate. See it?"

"It's a dog, Charlie. Just a dog. Must be a stray." Though I had to admit it had given me the willies too to see it moving down there. "Look, it's just picking through the scraps down by the bin. Can you see? It's not a wolf." I was speaking as gently as I could, trying not to sound patronizing. But I mean, how old was she?

"It's trying to fool you. It'll come into the yard. Into the house."

"No it won't. I'll shut the gate. Right now."

"No!" She clung to me like a drowning man. "Don't go down. It'll get you!"

It was time to be firm. I disengaged myself with difficulty, held her wrists away from me. "Charlotte," I said—and I never say that unless I'm being serious—"don't be stupid. I'll shut the gate, and then, wolf or no wolf, it won't get in. Watch from the window. I'll be right back. And stop sniveling or you'll wake Mum."

I was as good as my word. I went down to the yard: there was no wolf there. I went across to the gate and looked up and down the alley. Nothing bit me, though the air did nip through my pajamas. The bin had been knocked over but there was no sign of the dog. I shut the gate and locked it. As I went back I glanced up at Charlie's window, but she wasn't looking out to see her brother's heroism.

"Okay. All dealt with." I was back in her room. She was sitting on her bed, hunched over hugging her knees, eyes wide and bright in the darkness. "It's done. I locked the gate."

"Didn't you hear them?"

"Doing what?" I was fed up of asking questions. This was getting stupid.

"They were around the front. I heard them scratching."

"At the front door? Why didn't they just ring? Or knock. Come on, Charlie, it's the middle of the night. I'm really tired. Just leave it."

"But I heard them, I did. They were scratching to get in. They're never going to leave me, James, not till they get me."

"Bloody hell!" I was really angry now. "Let's see them then." And I was out of her room and down the stairs, despite her half-whispered plea to stop. I flung the front door open wide and stepped out into the street, ignoring the pavement freezing my feet. Nothing to be seen. I wheeled around and found Charlie standing in the doorway.

"Satisfied now? Come on, get inside." But she was

blocking the way, mutely pointing at the outside of the door. I stared at it, rubbing one foot on the other pajama leg to try and numb the cold.

"Charlie, it's always been scuffed."

"Not like that it hasn't. See the scratches?"

"No. Get out of the way. I'm freezing." I pushed past her and forcibly shut the door. "Now for Pete's sake, stop worrying. Nothing's going to hurt you." Rather to my surprise, Charlie seemed to take part of my advice to heart. She wasn't convinced, I could tell that much, but she appeared to have become quite fatalistic all of a sudden. She went upstairs to her room, put on the light, and went to sit on the bed. I sat down next to her, trying to be calming.

"The main thing is to get some sleep. Then you'll feel heaps better. You must feel lousy now: you certainly look bad."

"Thanks."

"If you sleep for a bit, you'll be better later. Then we can go out. We could go see a film if you want or there's that tatty fair on in the park. Whatever. We've not been out for ages. Mum's off out tomorrow, doing that course, so we can do what we want." I was burbling a bit; she may not have been knackered, but I was. "It'll be dawn soon, I'll make you a cup of tea when it's light. I'll just have a rest first. Budge up."

I lay down along the edge of her bed. She didn't protest. I think she was just pleased to have me there. I was past caring. In a few minutes, I was asleep.

Twenty-Six

I can't hold it off much longer. I can't stay awake. James is snoring alongside. Doesn't know how lucky he is. I can't put it off. They may as well have me.

I was too tired to write. The pen dropped from my hand and I let the notebook slide off my legs onto the bed. I got up one last time, walked over to the window. Outside, the sky was beginning to lighten. The house backs and yards were washed out, flattened by a single dark swathe of cold gray-blue. Everything was silent. No wolves were prowling here now. They were waiting for me in my dream.

It was then that I noticed the change. Something faintly bothered me, something that was not quite right nagged at my brain. It was so hard to concentrate; what was it—something I was seeing . . . ?

Yes. The view. The view of the yard was different from before. Subtly so. How it was different was hard to say. At first, the only thing I could be sure of was that it seemed more *complex* than it should ordinarily be.

Then I realized why, and it all made sense. There were trees outside the window where there had been none before. All along the alley, by the brick-walled yards and the backs of houses, they were clustering: tall, black, graceful forms with spreading branches that merged into the predawn sky.

It was not that they blocked out the normal view. They were neither in front of it nor behind it, but seemed to take up exactly the same space, coexistent. It was like when something goes wrong with a camera and you get two completely different photos superimposed on each other, each struggling for supremacy, each undercutting the other. So it was here. The forest and the street were merged.

I could still see the bathroom lights on in the house opposite, and even see the blurry shadow of a man moving behind the frosted glass. He was probably getting ready for an early shift, dousing himself in cold water or lathering up and feeling for his razor with eyes half closed. And yet in the very same space he occupied, a single heavy tree stood too, thickly needled branches filling the room. Its trunk seemed to rise from the floor below, spearing up across the lit space through the bathroom ceiling into the dark attic above and out through the roof into the night. The man's shadow shifted, he moved through the tree to get a towel. My head spun.

All along the back alley this merging was repeated, with

bricks and branches fighting for every inch of territory. A man walked along the shrouded cobbles with a cigarette burning between his lips, straight through a succession of trees. At the end of the alley, almost out of view, a car suddenly passed, carving a giant trunk like a knife through butter: butter that retained its form and closed up perfectly behind it.

My eyes watered—or were they crying? I couldn't tell. I simply remained looking out even as my eyes glazed and everything was blurred from view. I was in a forest, in a town. And I could not escape. The wolves had already broken through. Now the very trees had come to join them, jostling up against my window and seeking to blanket out the world. I could not escape. I recognized the trees themselves now. They were the same pines that I had chased through over twenty-four hours before, the last time I had slept. I had tried to evade them, to close out the chase and catch up with Max. But it was not to be. I was still in the wood and there was nowhere to hide.

After an unknown time I felt a stiffness in my legs and remembered where I was. I drew the curtains and came away from the window, instinctively walking around the gnarled mossy pine trunk that rose through the carpet beside the wardrobe. I sat down on the bed again under a dark canopy. The smell of pine sap filled the room. Sleep began to pull my limbs down hard as if lead weights fixed them to the bed. Through force of habit I wrenched myself into a sitting position, reaching out for my Walkman. But I let my hand drop. There was no point running any more. I lay down again, head on the pillow. James slept silently alongside.

As I slipped toward sleep, my thoughts rose up in the last moments with a kind of clarity. How strange it was that my pursuit of Max should make me, in turn, pursued. Once, back at the mill pool, I had been welcome too. The women in the water had sought to draw me in. But my refusal had angered them; now the guardians of that country would prevent me from catching up with Max—he who had accepted and passed through.

Why had Kit not warned me of the dangers? Perhaps he was angry too: I had rejected the fruit. From beginning to end, I had failed to follow Max when it counted, coming close to him, never catching up. In short, I had messed up every chance I had.

I was too weary to feel the anguish my failure deserved. My eyes closed. The smell of the wood grew strong. My bed shifted, becoming sloped, uneven. Needles prickled my arms. Wolves howled.

Twenty-Seven

When I woke up, it was around eleven. Light was streaming in through the window. For a moment I was confused by my surroundings, but then I remembered that I was in Charlie's room. I'd been completely out of it. Hadn't dreamed a thing. To my great relief, Charlie was lying peacefully alongside me. At bloody last. The events of the night came flooding back to me, making no more sense than they had then. Less, if anything. *Wolves.* Christ.

At least Charlie was finally asleep. By the looks of her she'd be out for a long while. Very deeply asleep this time: no movements, no disturbances, no nightmares. Good. Still, Mum had better know. I got up and went downstairs.

No Mum, just a note on the kitchen table. I cursed roundly. Of course, she was away in town, away for the day on the secretarial course. She'd be back this evening. The note confirmed it. No number left. *Have a good time.* Oh well.

I had breakfast and got dressed, then looked in on Charlie again. Still flat out. The curtains had been left open and I went over to shut them. As I did so, I caught sight of a notebook lying on the carpet on the other side of the bed. There it was. Just like that.

A thrill of the forbidden passed through me. She would never know. I crept over and bent to pick up the notebook, keeping my eyes on Charlie's face the whole time. She didn't stir, her breathing made no sound. Spark out. I took the book and retreated downstairs to the kitchen table.

A single glance told me that there was far more of it than I expected. Charlie seemed to have been keeping up a diary for weeks, almost ever since Tilbrook had given it to her, and the book was three-quarters filled. It was all in her usual scruffy scrawl, hastily written in pen, although a lot of it was messy even by her standards. The first few entries were short, and so were the last—she seemed to have peaked midway. Well, I had nothing else to do, so I settled down for a read. It was only when I began that I realized the nature of the record.

Reading it took me half an hour—maybe more, because I kept going over bits again to try and make sense of them. There wasn't much sense to be found. What I did make out was that my little sister was very, very confused.

It was a diary of her dreams and, from what I could gather, those dreams had been spinning her a yarn for weeks and weeks, ever since the time she went back to the pool. All those hints she'd given me in that period, all the doubts I'd had, now stood in sharp relief, revealed as the tips of a massive iceberg hidden under her quiet surface. Day by day we'd got on with ordinary drab things when it was all happening for her at night. And to think I'd quietly sat and listened to that bloody Dr. Tilbrook waffle on about her exploring her loss. Exploring was right! Poor Charlie.

The worst of it was it proved what I'd expected. Charlie simply hadn't accepted Max was gone. Well, she knew he'd *gone* all right, but she was still after him and her dreams were convincing her she was catching him too. And she seemed to be transferring her convictions to the real world, hanging around his poor mum and dad, hearing their son's voice, maybe seeing him into the bargain. But I didn't understand the wolves bit at all.

What should I do? Charlie was asleep and secure. That was the main thing, and she wasn't having nightmares or wounding herself now. Okay, let her sleep. Mum was away, but Dr. Tilbrook's number should be somewhere. I went to check out Mum's telephone book. Sure enough, there it was. Right, let's see what he had to say about this. *Exploring her loss*, my arse.

The phone rang and rang. Come *on*. Finally, a pick up. A woman's voice. *Sorry, Dr. Tilbrook is away this weekend. In London. Back on Monday. Why don't you call then?* Brilliant—thanks a lot. No, no message.

Useless. But all was not yet lost. Charlie would be asleep for a long while yet. With luck she wouldn't surface till Mum got back. She wouldn't be in any danger as long as she was comatose and as long as I watched over her. When reinforcements arrived, we could work out what to do.

I stockpiled a couple of bags of crisps and a can of Coke from the kitchen and nabbed the biscuit tin for good measure. All this I took to my room. Then I poked my nose into Charlie's: no change there. Satisfied that all was well, I retreated to my bedroom, leaving both our doors wide open. I assembled a pile of comics and a few books I'd never got round to reading and settled down in comfort. For the moment, all I could do was wait and see what happened.

Twenty-Eight

I let my head fall back, and lifted my throat up ready to be bitten. I might as well get it over with.

But nothing happened. No teeth, no fetid breath, no howling. I opened my eyes slowly. Pine tree branches clogged the view above. There was no wolf at my throat. Blinking a little, I raised my head and squinted around. It was the same slope that I had fallen down the day before, but now revealed in full by strong sunlight drifting down through the forest's dusty layers. And there, at the crest of the slope, stood the wolves, looking down at me.

They didn't seem any less savage. Even as I looked, two of them made a feint down the slope, growling, as if to leap and tear me apart. But something made them stop, turn back and return to the top of the rise. And I could see that the eyes of the group were as often turned to the right, out of my vision, as they were to me.

Suddenly a loud crash sounded from the right and the

wolves started. A second crash came, the sound of a heavy blow on wood. At this, without a noise or hesitation, the wolves turned tail and disappeared among the trees. I waited a little but they did not return.

Getting painfully to my feet, I took stock of the situation. More crashes resounded from the forest: repetitive, deliberate chopping. This was something I had never heard before in all my travels, and if the wolves feared it, then that was good enough cause to investigate. I would go that way.

I headed off along the side of the slope and almost immediately saw the source of the noise. Across an open space a man was cutting at a tree with an ax. He hewed away at it ceaselessly, never pausing or breaking his rhythm. At every stroke, fragments of white heartwood leaped into the air. The clearing was filled with the rough bright stumps of newly felled trees.

The man himself was tall and slim with long fair hair reaching to his shoulders. He didn't seem to have noticed me and I began to make my way among the stumps to greet him. But then I paused. In his thinness he reminded me strongly of Kit, but there was another resemblance too that awoke very different memories. Something about his thin white shoulders and his pale arms and the swirl of his long, long hair reminded me of the women in the pool.

Kit had called Max fortunate and said he was lucky to have been chosen. Maybe, but I was tied to the remembered terror of those moments, to the memories of black-green eyes approaching through the water, to the caressing touch of long cold fingers and the ripping of my flesh. And of Max sinking in their arms. Foolish or not, I did not want to meet this man. I left him to his work.

Sounds of other axes met my ears. I walked along the edge of the clearing and presently saw others chopping at trees, cutting the felled trunks into manageable logs and loading them onto carts. The forest all around was noticeably less dense than I remembered it, and up ahead I thought to see open patches of bright green showing through the trees.

At this I hastened forward, desperate to be out of the trackless forest at last. As I was about to leave the clearing and plunge into the last barrier of wood, I passed close to a woman gathering brushwood into a large woven basket. She looked up at me and smiled.

"Late for the fair? Keep on straight, love. It's not long now."

I hurried on without thanks. My heart had been given a jolt when I looked at her, so strongly did it remind me of the women in the water: the long hair, the smooth face, the green eyes. Her hair was blond, not pale green like theirs, and her skin had a healthy summer's tan. Still, it unnerved me.

Now I was among the outlying trees of the forest, running as best I could, with all the aches and grazes of the journey stiffening every joint and sinew. Strong, unadulterated light began to break upon my forehead, my eyes blinked at the sudden change and with a last impatient effort I broke through the final ragged clump of thorns and bushes, and was out into the open.

And here I stopped and gazed.

I had come out at the top of a gentle slope that appeared to mark the boundary of the great forest. On either side, the trees' edge stretched in a hard straight line into the hazy distance, following the crest of the rise. And out in front, stretching down from the wooded margin along all its immense length, was a sweet meadow bathed in summer sun. Long grasses waved in the sunshine, studded all over with red and yellow flowers. Butterflies of a hundred colors floated above the grass tips and bees hummed in the heavily scented air. After a month lost in the endless forest it was a sight to gladden the soul.

And this was only the beginning. The slope stretched down from me for a considerable distance, until—perhaps half a mile distant and a few hundred feet below—it leveled out to a great field or plain. This continued unbroken to the very horizon, except in a single place where a solitary green hill rose up. And at the foot of that hill, spread out exposed for me to gaze and marvel at, was the Great Fair.

Throughout all the later stages of my journey, Kit's words about the fair had been lodged clearly in my mind. "A *most marvelous and exotic fair.*" My eagerness to see it for myself had since been exceeded only by my desire to catch up with Max. And now the fair was revealed.

The nearest fringe of the fair extended right up to the foot of the slope on which I was standing. It was marked by a wooden fence or palisade, which surrounded the whole site and which was broken in many places by carved gateways decorated with green bunting. In a couple of places the fence had not been completed: carts laden with logs for this purpose were trundling down the slope from the forest and little crowds of workmen were swarming like beetles over the unfinished sections, sawing, hammering, driving new sections into the ground.

Through every gateway, people were streaming in and out, carrying baskets, pulling or pushing carts, or bearing bundles in their arms. Once inside, they melted into a sea of figures, a hive of motion, surrounding an endless fragmented patchwork of multicolored stalls, decked out with flags and waving streamers. At this distance, it was impossible to say what treasures the stalls contained, but the hubbub of the fair rose clearly up the slope to me, a beguiling mix of music, laughter, and general kerfuffle exactly as Kit had foretold.

At the center of the fair, the stalls gave way to great marquees, striped and fat, their roofs billowing slightly in the wind. Here too were dark towers of polished wood. They had openings at the top and gleaming slides spiraling around the outside. After a moment I realized what they were: helter-skelters of great size. Alongside these were raised, square platforms a bit like boxing rings and several open areas, laid with polished wood. I wondered what purpose these might serve—and then I remembered the great dance.

Somewhere below, amid the throng, was Max. I was closer to him than ever before and, although I could not be sure, it seemed to me that the fair was only gearing up and had not properly begun. Surely the dance could not yet have taken place? With a thrill of hope, I set off down the slope.

As I went, the long grasses brushed ceaselessly against my legs, stroking a sweet fragrance up around me. My path disturbed an endless succession of bright blue-and-red butterflies, which erupted up from the grass and were left dancing behind on either side. Several times giant rabbits or hares ran startled from the undergrowth, racing away from me up the slope. And high above, birds drifted and swooped against the sky, hunting insects on the winds. Onward, down the hill I went, possessed by a new delight, a resurrected energy. This was a run to awake in me the joy of living; gone was the deathly tiredness of the last few days, the dreary death-in-life of my dreary room and house and street. Gone was the muddled searching through the decaying town, picking among the grim scraps that Max had left behind. Gone too were the wearisome witterings of my brother and mother; as I ran, the choking fug their talk had left inside my brain was whipped into life by the swift air, teased out into thin shreds and scattered in my wake. My head was clear, my eyes shone, I was fully alive once more. Down the hill I ran, toward the waiting fair.

As I drew nearer, my eyes widened in increasing wonder at the beauty and richness of the stalls and their customers.

I could see now that even the meanest awnings were made of the finest silk and that the poles that held them up were painted gold. Meadow flowers had been plaited into long, slender bundles which looped merrily around the edges of each stall roof and around the sharp tops of each log in the palisade. Hanging too from the tallest poles on many stalls were ornate gold cages in which sat delightful songbirds of a thousand colors, all on their feet and singing plaintively at me as if their hearts would break.

This splendor was matched by the appearance of the visitors to the fair. I was now approaching one of the gates, to which a steady stream of people also headed. Men, women, and children—all wore the most colorful fabrics, mainly of green, yellow, and blue cloth. The women and children had long loose skirts with flowers in their hair. The men wore jaunty tunics and trousers; some sported broad-brimmed hats, others let their hair fall long around their shoulders. All went barefoot, talking and laughing excitedly together as they hurried toward the entrance of the fair.

Work on the palisade was now completed and the workmen flung down their tools and withdrew inside the compound. The tides of people flowing into the various gateways began to lessen into a fast dwindling trickle. A few latecomers were running toward the entrances, adults pulling children by their hands to speed them on or lifting them bodily into their arms. I was still running down the slope toward the nearest gate. Now the music from inside began to swell, reaching a new level of excitement and urgency. The noise of the crowd beyond the fence also grew, peals of laughter sounded, cries of joy and celebration. I was now too low down to see above the barrier—only the tops of the nearest stalls remained in view and presently these too disappeared behind the garlanded spikes.

I was running as hard as I could. There was hardly anyone remaining with me outside the barrier; only a few latecomers racing along with anxious faces, heads down. One of the last, a man, turned his head toward me and beckoned urgently.

"Come on! Come on!"

Then I saw it was Kit. He gestured toward the gate where a heavy door of bound logs, which had been concealed inside, was slowly swinging into position. I redoubled my efforts. Now I was at the bottom of the slope, I had joined the beaten path where lately so many people had walked. But I was all alone. The gate was almost shut. Kit disappeared inside without a backward glance. He was the last. I ran as hard as I could. I was the only one left outside. I ran, ran. The door closed to and I was still beyond the barrier.

And as it shut, all the noise—the music, the crying of the birds, the baying laughter of the people that had beaten down upon me like a water torrent so that I thought my back would break—all that engulfing cacophony was suddenly cut off.

In that terrible silence, I fell against the wood, pushing at it, banging at it, rubbing the skin from the base of my fists, beating against it until all my energy was gone. But the door remained fast.

I slumped to the ground outside the gate. The fair had begun, and I was still outside.

Twenty-Nine

I had eaten all the crisps and drunk the Coke, and had put away most of the biscuits. I had gone through the comics, too, and was now flicking through a cheesy fantasy novel that ripped off several I'd read before. Meanwhile, I'd been lounging on my bed with my head propped against the wall. So I was bloated, bored, and had a pain in my neck. And that was before my troubles began.

It was only luck that I knew anything about it at all. What with my sugary diet over the last few hours I was beginning to get a bit twitchy, and this finally propelled me out of my room to go downstairs and maybe look for something healthy to eat, or just watch *Grandstand* or something.

So I struggled to my feet and trudged out on to the landing. Here I listened carefully. No sound from Charlie's room. Good, she was still out cold. The longer that continued the better. I made for the stairs quietly, swung around the corner, and nearly died of fright.

There was a figure at the foot of the stairs.

My panic mechanisms were working, that was for sure. I gasped, my hair stood up, a cold shock cut a swathe across my body and my heart nearly burst out through my mouth—and all that before my eyes took in what I was seeing and I realized it was my own sister with her back to me.

But that was bad enough, to be honest. The worst of it was that she was utterly silent, slowly descending the final stair with the stealth of a murderer and the tread of a ghost. She was moving oddly, with movements that were at one and the same time eerily fluid and peculiarly jerky. Something was very wrong. It gave me a thrill of horror to realize that she must have left her room and gone across the landing, right outside my door, with me there all the time, completely unaware.

I could not see her face, but something irrational made me feel that I did not truly want to.

But wait, she was still my sister, for God's sake. There was no sense in acting like a fool. I called her, softly, with a slightly shaky voice.

"Hey, Charlie."

No answer. She did not turn or even pause. She gave no sign that she had heard a thing. She moved off along the hall, out of sight, with the same slow steps. I shook myself out of my frozen reverie and went down the stairs with a jerkiness of my own, born of uncertainty and fear.

"Charlie, where are you going?"

No response.

"How long have you been up?"

She was almost at the door now and I was still hovering like an idiot at the foot of the stairs. I realized that I was actually reluctant to catch up with her. Then I saw her reach out for the door latch. That stirred me up a little. She wasn't going out, not if I could help it, not after what I'd read. Maybe she thought she was off to one of Max's old hunting grounds again. Well, not if I could stop her.

So do something about it then! I half ran down the hallway and caught up with her, just as she began to step through the door.

"Charlie!"

I put my hand on her shoulder from behind. It was like touching a lump of meat: there was no response, no turning of the head. I pushed past her on to the pavement and looked her full in the face. And felt the cold shudder cut through me again.

Her face was very, very pale. Even her lips seemed bloodless. And her eyes, which were wide open, were looking right through me as if she were trying to see something far off, down at the end of the road or farther still, and I was directly in its path. She was frowning with great concern, but it had nothing at all to do with me or my touching her.

"Charls, snap out of it. What are you doing? You shouldn't be out. Come inside."

I let out a stream of blather like that, more for my own benefit than for hers. She wasn't paying attention in any case. She was still walking, one slow step after another, down the street, brows furrowed. Every now and then, she raised her head and looked—or made the appearance of looking—up at a point at roughly the height of the first-floor windows. And there was nothing to see there, nothing at all.

I was walking alongside her, reluctant to touch her again. We passed a couple of women gossiping in the road. They looked at us with blank distrust: at the girl walking robotlike along the road with a boy whispering at her shoulder.

Every now and then her eyes made a swift movement, making a little sudden roll or swiveling up or down. And it was this that told me the truth at last—and what a fool I'd been for not realizing at once: my sister was still asleep.

She was sleepwalking.

I stopped the chatter immediately. That would do no good, and it might do harm—I seemed to remember hearing that you should never wake a sleepwalker under any circumstances. Well, fine, but what the hell *were* you supposed to do? I had absolutely no idea.

I was extra-agitated because of what I'd read in Charlie's diary. Ten to one she was dreaming again, hunting Max through some wolf-infested jungle. What if she thought I was a wolf and attacked me if I touched her?

This was stupid. Our front door was still wide open behind us. Anyone could just walk in. I had to get us back.

I reached out and, stooping a little, took Charlie's right hand in my own. It was icy cold. Grasping it firmly, I put my left arm around her waist from the back and got a grip in her belt. Then I applied the brakes, leaning back and swiveling on my heels as I did so. It was like dancing a quickstep or something: Charlie was swung right round to face back up the street. And she didn't break the rhythm of her steps but carried on walking that same slow trudge, only this time back toward the house.

This counted as a success. I kept my hold, guiding her along, ignoring the looks I got from the two women as we passed again. Charlie seemed to be still asleep but, glancing at her face, I saw that her frown had deepened.

Back at the house, another swivel, another quickstep, and in through the door. No point trying to get upstairs. The lounge would have to do. Along the hall, one-two-three, and turn—in through the door and into the lounge. Quick kick-step behind me, slam the door to. The sound was louder than I'd intended. Charlie gave a little falter, and uttered a sound—half word, half groan. Her eyelids flickered, her face grimaced a little. I guided her around to the sofa and, still holding her by the waist, sat myself down so that she was forced to follow. Then I disengaged myself and stood up, letting her sink back into a sitting position. The twitches of her eyes and face grew more pronounced. She muttered something I couldn't catch.

"Charlie?"

Another mumble.

"Charlie. Wake up, lovey; it's James."

"Mmm."

"Come on, wake up."

Her eyes closed. Now they flickered open again, unfocused on me or on anything else.

"Charls?"

"Carnfinaway."

"What?" I bent closer, trying to catch it.

"Carn finda way in. M'looking. Carn findaway . . ." The eyes closed again. The breathing became slower, deeper. She was asleep once more.

In an instant I was back in the hall where I shut the door and bolted it, top and bottom. I grabbed Mum's mortise key from the plant stand and turned that in the lock for good measure. Then I rushed back through the lounge to the kitchen and bolted the back door too. Safe as houses. No more walking the street for Charlie now.

I was worn out. I needed some backup, but Mum's course would last all afternoon. It was about four now, so I probably had another couple of hours to go, maybe three. I had to knuckle down and wait.

The next two hours were dreadful. For a start, I wasn't able to turn on the TV because that would have woken Charlie. I couldn't use the one in Mum's room either because I didn't want to leave Charlie alone. Sleeping or not, I didn't trust her an inch. So I was forced to go on reading that rubbish novel. I sat in the easy chair, flicking the pages, unable to concentrate, keeping one eye always on Charlie's head lolling on the top of the sofa. The afternoon wore on, and the light outside began to fail. Still Mum didn't come back, and still Charlie slept on.

With all the shocks and stresses I'd endured, I was feeling a little flaky, and at around six-thirty a pain in my stomach informed me that it was time for food. I duly retired to the kitchen and ferreted around for the best it could offer, which turned out to be a tin of tuna heated with instant sauce and plonked on pasta. It didn't take long to prepare, maybe five minutes at most, and I kept the connecting door into the living room wide open so that I could hear if anything stirred. With my feast ready, I returned to the living room with it on a tray, hoping that the smell might force its way into Charlie's nostrils and bring her back to life.

And she was gone.

She was gone. The sofa was empty, the room was empty and the sash window to the side passage was wide open with a slight wind rippling its thin curtains.

I panicked.

I dropped the tray. I leaped over to the window and stuck my head out and looked to the left, as far as I could see around into our yard. Then I raced around to the back door and began hunting for the key that I thought was in my pocket, swearing and double-checking even when I knew it wasn't. Then I began hunting for it, running around and around the kitchen, when all the time I should have been out of the window after her and halfway down the road.

I found the key behind the empty pasta packet, and with more cursing and fumbling got the backdoor open and ran out into the yard. The gate was wide open.

Out in the alley there was no sign of her either, right or

left. Some kids were playing ball two doors up. Young kids, didn't know their names. I ran over.

"Here, have you seen a girl come out this way? About five minutes ago?"

The kids looked at me with blank, startled faces. They didn't answer yes or no, just looked. They were the stupidest kids I had ever seen. I controled myself with difficulty and attempted an ingratiating smile. It made a small one cry. But the biggest one, a blotchy boy with something brown smudged on the side of his face, finally summoned up the gumption to nod his head.

"You have? Where? Which way did she go?"

He pointed. I was down the alley in a flash and they were probably still gawping at me in silence when I turned the corner at the end.

As I came out into the street and was faced with another choice, a sudden horrible thought struck me: had Charlie taken her bike? If so, I was doomed. She probably hadn't—you couldn't sleep-cycle, could you? But then a second dismal thought struck: I should have taken *my* bike! James, you bloody fool! I was panicking still. Should I go back to get it or should I not? Then I saw our next-door neighbor, Mrs. Mortimer, heading across the road to me.

"Mrs. Mortimer, have you seen Charlie? She's gone out and her mum wants her."

"I passed her just now, dear. White as a sheet. Never quite recovered from—*you know*—I suppose. But who would, poor thing?"

"Did you see where she was heading?"

"A dreadful experience for a mite. You'd never get over it, not really. Poor thing, yes, she passed me on the corner of Cottonmill Road. She'll be off to the fair. Lots of her friends going I expect. Oh, bye then, and say hello to your mother from me!"

I was running now, down the road to the Cottonmill corner. All thought of my bike was discarded; I only had two blocks to run, and I knew where I was going. The fair in the New Park. I'd forgotten all about it. And Charlie had mentioned looking for a fair in the diary of her dreams. It was perfectly possible that she might confuse the two, go hunting in the New Park for memories of Max. Perfectly possible. And anything might happen to her in the state she was in—half asleep, hallucinating, and worse.

I cut the corner off, ducking down the alley behind the last row of houses, trying to make up time.

It didn't work out like that.

Dusk had fallen and the sky was black with clouds, except for a yellow-red smear up ahead. The alley was in deep shadow and a few lights were on in the houses on either side. There was no one around. When I had got about halfway up, I saw a couple of stray dogs nosing about in the entrails of a ruptured bin bag. As I drew near, they stopped their rootling, raised their heads, and stared. They were big dogs, Alsatians maybe. I increased my speed, hoping to get by quickly, but to my dismay they left the mess of bones and tins and began to run alongside, keeping pace with me.

Bloody strays. I tried to ignore them, but they were much closer than I liked. All of sudden, one of them darted out, snapping at my feet. I skidded to a halt and kicked out at it, missing by a mile. And then both dogs began to bark with unbridled fury, blocking the way, filling the alley with the fury of their sound.

The second one made a lunge for my ankle. I pulled back just in time and backed off to the side of the alley, looking from side to side for help. No one was near and there were no lights visible in the houses opposite. This was bad: the dogs were barking furiously, making little feints at my legs and backing away only when I kicked out.

Out of the corner of my eye, I spied a long thin piece of metal lying on the ground among the grassy cobbles. An old railing, a meter long. I edged my way toward it, back to the wall, keeping my eyes firmly on the dogs. Closer and closer I went. Still the dogs were circling. At last the edge of the metal touched my shoe. I kicked out wildly and, as my assailants fell back, bent down, grabbed the rail and straightened, all in one smooth movement. I stood there against the bricks, swinging it back and forth in front of me like a cudgel.

The nearest dog crept close. I could see the spittle on its lips, see its green eyes glinting in the dusk.

It leaped forward, jaws open. I swung the railing down with all the force I could muster. It caught the dog's shoulder, driving it down with a squeal against the cobblestones. Then it leaped up and began racing around in circles in a paroxysm of yelping and barking, limping madly and frothing at the mouth. The other dog made a halfhearted lunge at me but my blood was up. I slashed out at it, narrowly missing the side of its head, and it turned and ran off up the alley.

The injured dog was still obsessed with its own woes, running round and round as if it wanted to chase and devour itself. I slipped away and ran on. Thirty seconds later, with my ears ringing from the howling that echoed up the alley, I was down a side passage and out under the streetlamps again. And directly opposite, across the road, was the New Park.

There was a hand-painted banner up on the railings beside the gate.

NEW PARK AUTUMN FÊTE—TODAY
Entrance £1

A small queue of chilly people were lined up on the pavement, waiting to pay at a couple of tables positioned just inside. Beyond the railings, a whole sea of little stalls had been erected, gaudily illuminated by multicolored lights hung from the trees. Grainy rock music issued from a few loudspeakers on poles and half the town seemed to be milling about below. I could not see if Charlie was among them.

I took my place in the queue. The woman in front, who had a small girl in tow, frowned and ushered her child as far away from me as possible. It was only then that I realized I was still holding the cudgel. I quietly dropped it inside the railings.

When I got to the tables I paid my pound to a long-haired bloke in a leather jacket, who sat hunched over his money tin as if it gave him warmth.

"Excuse me," I said. "I'm looking for my sister. She's about my height, she's got blue jeans, a green—"

"You think I'd remember? Don't be stupid—one pound, mate." He'd already turned to the next in line. The man behind pushed me forward beyond the tables into the fête.

And I stood there, like those kids in our alley, gazing stupidly at the silhouettes of a mass of people milling about sluggishly around the stalls under the hanging lights. Hundreds of thronging people, laughing too loudly, desperately intent upon having fun. And somewhere among them perhaps was Charlie, lost from me and losing herself.

The latent panic that had been in my chest ever since I found her gone burst to the surface, and with it came the tears. Everyone around me was too big, too loud, too brash, and careless of my search. I was alone. I could not call her, I could not see further than a few feet. Somewhere among the crowded stalls, she must be wandering vacant-eyed, oblivious to everything, seeking Max.

And suddenly I was hit by the great fear that I had been denying to myself all this time. A terror that my sister might succeed in her desire, that she might just be reunited with her best friend Max that very night.

Tears ran down my cheeks as I elbowed my way into the crowd.

Thirty

At first, when I was in one place only, despair threatened to overwhelm me.

I was slumped against the closed door. Night was falling and cold stars were coming out overhead. There was a terrible accusing silence all around. Yet I knew that inches from me, beyond the barrier of wood, the Great Fair blazed with life.

I was just in one place, sitting on the earthen floor outside the palisade. And at that moment I had no hope, no way to turn. Far off, the band of forest at the top of the slope turned black against the sky. I was hunched up, resting my face on my knees.

After a while, I got slowly to my feet and begun to trudge around the fence perimeter, gazing up at the sharp points of the endless stakes, each one twice my height and ceramic-smooth. There was not a chance of scaling them.

I do not know how long I walked the circumference of

the fence. My mind drifted, thinking of Max and how long it was since I had looked him in the face. I did not concentrate on where I went. I may have turned back the way I had come, once or several times, I don't know. At one point I came to another of the fair's entrances. This too was securely barred. I scarcely bothered to test it, my mind was so numb, my despair so great.

At last my feet gave way, tripping over a discarded chunk of wood. I fell heavily against the fence, and collapsed there finally into a sitting position, head to one side, hands limply in my lap.

Until that precise moment, I had been in one place only. Then, suddenly, I was not. My vision seemed to swim and the darkness grew a little paler. I groaned.

"Charlie?"

A familiar voice close by. There was a shadow in front of me, bending slightly, still out of focus, surrounded by a whole series of obscure blotches and streaks of color. It said something I couldn't catch. I tried very hard to listen and to make the figure out. I narrowed my eyes.

"Charls?"

All of a sudden I saw. It was my brother, standing there as large as life on the trodden grass outside the Great Fair, bending forward with his hands on his knees looking at me.

"Can't find a way," I said.

"What?" He was as stupid as ever.

"I can't find a way in. I'm looking, but it's impossible. I can't find the way." He frowned and faded. The spattering of lights and colors that had surrounded him disappeared too, and I was just looking out across the plain into the dusk.

Perhaps I slept then, I don't recall, but after an unknown time I suddenly became aware of myself again and found I was in two places at once, sitting on the sofa in my old home while still resting against the palisade. I could feel both the hardness of the wood and the sagging softness of the leather against my back and shoulders. Directly in front of me, the endless plain stretched away and the living room window looked out on to our neighbor's wall.

There was no difference in strength between the two worlds. They coexisted. The ground in front of me was both half-trodden grass and the moldy old carpet that Mum couldn't afford to replace. There was a faint radiance emanating from behind me that lit up that ground and I could not tell whether it was caused by the illuminations of the fair or our kitchen light. Perhaps it was both.

I had been sitting there for a little while, looking at nothing in particular, before I realized what I had to do. It came to me suddenly, like a lightning flash of hope amid the blackness all around, and I knew that it was my last chance.

All this time I had been searching for Max alternately in both worlds but I had never, or almost never, had the chance to operate in them both at once. I had had to start from scratch each time, hunting in the forest, or seeking Max out in our shared places in town. And though, in my world, I'd almost found him several times, each time getting closer than the last, something had always thwarted me. But now the two worlds were fused and I was right on the edge of the fair, closer to Max than I had ever been. Perhaps now, if I let myself be guided by my dual vision, I could harness the clues both worlds gave me and find a way through.

For the moment, there was no point concentrating on the world of the fair: I had run up against a barrier there. So I must grit my teeth and focus on the other, the old and shabby world, and see where it took me.

I was beyond thinking, I must be guided. And right ahead of me was the window.

First I must escape. Cautiously, I looked over my shoulder. I saw solid wood and the view toward the kitchen door. The light was on in there: I could hear someone moving about, clanking pans and cupboard doors. It was time for me to slip away. I got to my feet, unsure whether I was treading on carpet or grass. Then I walked unsteadily toward the window. It wasn't easy going at first. I kept looking too far ahead, at the dim expanse of the plains, and consequently nearly walked bang into the wall.

Fortunately, when I found the handles, the sash opened upward smoothly and without a sound and I was able to climb through. Then I set off down the side-passage, through our yard, out into the alley and away—down the street, across the plains. Easy.

The strange thing is that as soon as I started moving, I knew the direction I had to go. Not consciously, but quite clearly, as if a voice were calling me from somewhere up ahead, directing me at every junction or place of doubt. At all times, the dual perspective remained: I passed by lines of houses, clumps of trees, roads with moving cars and hummocks of grass covered with discarded carts and piles of logs. Often I passed people too, always from the drabber world, walking the pavements instead of the meadows. Their faces were curiously indistinct and shadowy to me and I did not look at them.

It was nighttime in both worlds, and this helped my progress because it ironed out the worst of the differences and blended the two together in a gray-black mass. One curious exception was the effect of the streetlights that I passed. Whenever I came alongside one, the walls and the pavements bathed by its glow sprang out with great clarity, dampening down the glimpses of the meadow within the cone of light. Once I passed out of its pool, the street picture sprang back instantly to become the neutral equal of the darkened field. When cars passed, their headlamps briefly bisected the darkness, illuminating moving triangles of road and building which quickly disappeared from view, to be replaced by a deeper, double-layered darkness.

The sounds of the worlds blended also: I could hear cars passing but only faintly and always slightly distorted, as if I were listening from under water. Similarly, noises of owls calling from nearby trees sounded muted, echoing and strange.

In this manner, moving slowly and with great care, I

progressed through the two worlds at once. Nothing hindered me, nothing frightened me, no wolves, no cars, no nothing. I felt myself safe, suspended between the dangers of each place. And all the time, something undefined guided me and called me on.

Then, right ahead, I saw that I had not been mistaken in my hope. I saw what I was looking for. The fusion of the two worlds: a new gateway to the fair.

Perhaps it was always there, that tiny forgotten door in the endless palisade, perhaps I had even passed it already in my wanderings. But I would never have found it without the linking of the two worlds.

My path had taken me out into the darkening meadows, away from the great fence, following the vague zigzag patterns of the spotlit streets. For much of this time, I had lost sight of the fair altogether, submerged into the dusk behind me. But now I saw the fence ahead of me once more. The road that I was following led straight toward it, through the grasses toward a blurry point of light. I hastened forward and as I drew near, saw that the great smooth spikes of the palisade now shared their space with a second barrier, a ring of black metal railings that faded away on either side of the single lit space.

Now I was nearer still, and the diffuse smear of light coalesced into a series of concrete images. There was a gap in the railings, a wide one, with light spilling through it to illuminate the neat hopscotch slabs of the pavement outside. Beside it, in an indefinite huddle of half shapes, was a line of people, ghost-frail and see-through, stretching away to one side. I saw them, but took no notice, for here too, in precisely the same place, was a door in the smooth log wall, a simple gap where two great staves had been cut off at ankle height, leaving a hole to step through.

And beyond it was a blur of color and movement, the true source of the light that jetted out and bruised my face where I stood in the darkness.

I was standing still now, gazing at the vision with open mouth. And suddenly a weaker beam of light fell on me from the left. I half glanced to my side, barely caring, and saw two orbs of ugly neon yellow racing toward me, turning the meadow in its path to flashing tarmac as it came. And some distant memory came looping down to me over the fence of my absorption and told me I must run.

And run I did, toward the gap.

There was a whirl of noise and motion. I felt the car pass close behind, saw the gap loom up at great speed as I ran. Distorted voices cried out, faceless images turned toward me and stretched out clawing hands to bar my way. I ran at full speed, head down, fists clenched, and as the final figure rose up, vast and menacing, I closed my eyes tight shut and leaped into the light.

Thirty-One

I passed through the gap into a place of light and noise. With my blinded eyes closed, my ears deafened, I landed on solid earth and charged forward pell-mell. I barged through a mass of bodies, sensing repeated contact but feeling nothing.

As I ran, my ears adjusted to a whirl of sound: I heard an overlapping of voices, shouts, whisperings, snatches of music, scufflings, and metallic clangs. They all seemed to fall in upon each other and cancel each other out. The noise faded to a muffled undercurrent. My eyes grew accustomed to the light. I came to a gradual halt and raised my head to the world around.

I was standing in the midst of a marvelous confusion, the place where fairs from two worlds met and mingled. And though they existed separately, I saw that they interacted with a chaotic harmony that was entirely lacking beyond their boundaries.

First, there were the people of the fairs. They walked among—and through—each other with a fluid ease, each crowd a reflection and extension of the other. I could not make out faces clearly, but I could see among them children of the town and of the forest, some holding ice creams or candy-floss, others strange tangles of black and red threads frozen in a latticed ball and fixed on the end of sticks. With them walked the adults, among them familiar men and women from the terraces and back alleys. These were dwarfed and made dumpy by the slender people from the forest, all willowy grace and sinew and long straight hair. Back and forth and through and through, the seas of people wove their way around each other, and crashing waves of noise I barely heard broke endlessly upon me.

I began to weave my way through the crowds and found that both layers of people steered around me as I went. Alone of all the multitude, I walked in both fairs; with every step, I brushed past crinkled anoraks, woolly sweaters, silken tunics, bare brown arms.

On either side, rising like cliffs above the flood of heads, the stalls and tents displayed their wares. They mixed the familiar and the strange: tarpaulined coconut shies and rifle ranges overlapped with gaudy booths where laughing long-haired men and women threw silver balls at bulb-shaped pots suspended from the trees. If a pot was broken, a reward fell to earth—a shower of coins, a strip of silk, a living bird tied to a stone.

The stall roofs were covered with the ephemera of the fairs: mingled balloons and birdcages, streamers and loudspeakers, weather-stained canvases and fine-striped silk. I paused by a contraption of wood and springs, where children were placed in cushioned baskets and tossed in arcs from one side of a giant seesaw to another. This was superimposed on an open-sided caravan where a man and woman sold hot dogs and steaming soup to a chilly crowd. A constant stream of other delights flowed past me. A bear danced by, then a woman selling choc-ices, next a man spinning along in a wheel of bone. My eyes were saucer-shaped, dazzled by it all.

But I had not forgotten him, not quite. I still remembered why I had come here and for whom. All this time, my eyes were peeled and scanning, this way and that, searching the crowd for Max.

A tall man with a broad-brimmed hat, narrow eyes, and a wide smile swooped in front of me, offering bags of sweets from a tray. I could not tell which world he was from. I shook my head, he shrugged, still smiling, whirled round behind me, and was gone. A woman walked past on stilts, throwing confetti on those below. It fell on my shoulders like red and yellow rain.

Max was nowhere to be seen. I moved on into a place where games were being played. The rivers of people swept tightly around the margins of an open area, where rusty bumper cars and bite-sized roundabouts vied with the team sports of the people of the forest, played with handheld colored hoops and long silver nets. I was crushed and buffeted among the pressing throngs, their eyes aflame with food, drink, and the heady delights of the night fair. Children of two worlds moved in front of me, faces smudged and absent—twice I started forward to accost the one I knew, twice I fell back thwarted as blank faces turned on me. I was wandering blindly among strangers. Max was not here among the crowds. I drifted farther on.

ii

I nearly got beaten up as I pushed my way through the New Park swarms. I was swinging my head from side to side like a madman, craning round people's shoulders to see if Charlie was beyond them, not looking where I was going. So I soon collided with someone and of course it was a massive bloke with a studded jacket. He wheeled around before I could say anything.

"Look where you're going."

"Sorry."

"You stupid or something? You'd better apologize a bit faster next time, sonny."

"Yes, sorry."

I let the crowd pull me away and wandered miserably on. I couldn't see more than three feet in any direction. I hadn't a chance of finding Charlie. I might have passed her already if some fat sod had been standing in the way. I stumbled on between the rifle range and the raffle tent. Middle-aged ladies were buying tickets for bottles of wine and scented soaps. Crowds of boys shot guns at moving ducks, laughing at each other's miss. No sign of Charlie anywhere. My arms felt knotted with tension.

"James."

It took a couple of calls for me to hear and turn around. A boy from up our street.

"You looking for your sis?"

"Yeah. How d'you know?"

"I saw her bust in. You're not the only one looking for her. She mad or something?"

"What's she done?"

"Bust in without paying. Bloke from the fair went after her but didn't catch her far as I know. She must have been really moving."

"Bloody hell."

"Better catch her before he does, mate."

I didn't need telling. I plunged into the fray again, moving fast as I could, ducking and weaving, turning and looking. It was a nightmare—the yellow-red lighting and the thick pooling darkness turned everyone's faces inside out; I couldn't make out colors or features at all. So many kids, so many girls, all of her size, and her hair and her clothes, and moving, melting into each other so fast I couldn't be sure what I could see. It was a nightmare from one end of the fair to the other and I couldn't find my sister anywhere.

iii

As I walked deeper in and ever new wonders met my eyes, I became dimly aware that the balance between the two worlds had subtly altered—and that one level was fading from me. As I watched, the people of the town with their heavy coats pulled high against the cold began to grow fainter and more wraithlike. Slowly, smoothly, their outlines thinned and flickered, while those of the people of the forest became harder, stronger, fatter with color and definition. The town stalls faded too and, as they disappeared entirely, the delights of the Great Fair swelled with color and I heard for the first time the full force of its merry instruments and throats.

A man was sitting on a stool not far from me, surrounded by what looked like a mass of giant porcupine quills sticking into the earth. From each was suspended a paper lantern giving off a colored light. He saw me watching him and beckoned.

"Enjoying the fair, my love?" he asked me as I approached.

"Yes, very much," I said, stopping at the fringe of the forest of quills. Each one was very sharp at the tip. The nearest lantern cast green light upon my face.

"Take one to light your way," he said, gesturing with long fingers.

"I don't have any money," I said politely. He shook his head, smiling.

"Take one. Everything in the fair is free."

"I am looking for the Great Dance," I said. "Do you know where it will take place?"

"Up the hill of course, on the far side of the fair. You had better hurry."

"It hasn't started yet, has it?" I felt a thrill of panic.

"Soon. If you are going up the hill, you had best take a lantern."

I reached out and touched the nearest quill. A sharp pain pierced me and the lantern hanging from the end shuddered. I drew my hand back and inspected it: there was a drop of blood on my middle finger. The man on the stool was watching me with sharp eyes. Suddenly I wanted to get away. I turned and hurried into the crowd.

A few minutes more and the crowds around me had thinned considerably. I was walking slightly uphill, away from the center of the fair. A woman approached, leading a small infant by the hand. As I passed, the child turned its head and looked at me with huge expressionless green eyes. I dropped my gaze and hastened on.

A young man fell into step beside me.

"Where are you going, my dear?" he said.

"To the dance. Is this the way?"

"Yes, but you must hurry. Why do you go?"

"I am looking for a friend who will dance there."

"And you will dance too?"

"No . . . that's not why . . ." I became silent. It was hard to explain.

He laughed lightly. "Well, whyever you go, you haven't

much time. This year's dancers are all assembled, save one. The music will soon begin. Follow the lit way." Then he dropped back a little and was left behind.

I was almost out beyond the last few stalls, out of the ring of light and sound. Ahead was a path, lit by trees decked out with colored candles. It snaked its course up the steepening hill under the stars. I began to run, following the trail of illuminated trees.

iv

It was no good. I was worn out, ready to burst from frustration. I had searched the whole fête, for what it was worth, to no avail. I had to rest. I stopped beside a burger stand, where a man with tattooed arms was nudging pieces of meat across a hot plate. I was hungry. I'd never had my pasta. I paid my pound and stood quietly while the man put together a burger with too much onion. Then I propped myself against a caravan wall out of the main flow of traffic and ate it. It wasn't as hot as it looked.

I might have missed her in the fête, but somehow I didn't think so. She wasn't trying to hide; whether asleep or awake she was doing something all on her own and wasn't concerned about anyone else. If she'd been among the stalls I'd have found her by now.

So where was she? Somewhere in the New Park, but that didn't help me because it stretched out beyond the lit area of the fête in three directions, past playing fields and new plantations of trees up to the edge of the hill.

I'd never be able to find her now, at night. Hopeless.

I dropped the last bit of undercooked burger on the ground and wiped my hands on my trousers. She had come here for a reason—all I had to do was work out what it was. The fair had attracted her: she'd dreamed about Max in one. So why wasn't she here now?"

I thought back to what I'd read in her book. She'd spent a lot of time looking for him in their old haunts—down at his house, among the cars. Perhaps that's what she was doing again—hunting his ghost in places they'd shared.

Think, James, think.

Where would she go, trailing Max's memory? Where would Max be?

v

I had left the stalls behind me, following the line of trees uphill, across the black landscape and under the starry sky. The sounds of the fair were drowned in the great cloaking immensity of the night; all I could hear were my feet scuffing on the short tussocky grass.

The hill became very steep, but still the line of trees with their pools of light continued on unbroken. I found I was following a series of shallow steps cut in the grass to make the going easier.

I do not know how long it took me to reach the top of the hill. I was desperately aware of every step, of the grinding boundaries of every wrenching breath, and by the time I reached the top, my legs were shaking with exhaustion. At the brow of the hill I almost stopped, but tottered onward three more steps until I came to the last illuminated tree. Then I stopped dead.

A man and a woman stepped out from the darkness on either side and blocked the path. They both carried thin silver staffs in their hands.

"This way is barred," the woman said. She was very tall.

"The dance is about to begin," the man added.

"Please, I am looking for my friend," I said. "I think he has come this way."

"Too late," the woman said. "The way is barred to all save those who will dance."

"Turn back to the fair," said the man.

"But that is what I am here for!" I said. "I am here to dance too! Let me pass."

Neither answered, but only gazed down at me from where they stood, half in and half out of the colored pool of light conjured by the final tree.

"Please," I said again. "Let me pass. I am here to dance."

There was a long silence, then both smiled.

"Then welcome," said the woman. "You are expected. But you must lose no more time."

I felt a desperate joy. They drew apart and I started forth between them.

"Hurry," the man said. "The music is about to begin."

vi

I leaned against the caravan, trying to shut it all out,

thinking back to the notes I'd read in her book.

She'd even written down some of the places she was going to try. Where were they? One was Max's house. One was the scrapyard. But there were more too. I couldn't remember them.

I should have paid more attention to where she went with him . . . the steelworks, that was one. They'd gone there a lot, but that was on the other side of town from here. Not right. Somewhere else.

There were other places written in her book, I knew it. What were they? Think!

I walked along the side of the caravan and found myself on the edge of the fête. It was quieter here, easier to think.

Somewhere near here.

I spun around slowly where I stood, under the night sky, seeing the fair, the upstairs lights of the nearest houses, then the darkness of the park and the black hill outlined by the stars beyond. It was a clear, cold night.

And then suddenly I remembered. It hit me like a blow. I remembered where they used to go, up on the hill above the town.

I turned away from the lights and the crowds and the fair, and set off across the black grass toward the far edge of the park, toward the hill where the quarries are.

vii

A track led over the brow of the hill. I followed.

Behind me and below, lit by a hundred thousand

lanterns, was the marvelous tapestry of the fair. I never looked its way. My eyes were only for what lay ahead, suspended in a well of artificial light between two higher humps of ground.

The site of the Great Dance.

The path worked its way down the contours of the hill in a series of graceful curves. It ended at a trellis arch covered with vines, where six carved stone steps led down to the lip of a dance floor, open to the sky.

The dance floor was a vast circle of polished wood set into the side of the hill, lit by a hundred lanterns hanging from trees around its perimeter and most of all by a huge orb sat atop a giant pole planted at its very center. All around the edge beneath the trees stood a throng of people, a beautiful host of men and women with garlands in their hair. At the very far end, opposite the steps, rose a dais on which a group of musicians were sitting. They sat so far away that I could not make out their number nor the exact instruments they played, but the music that now struck up, which seemed a lilting melody of pipe and string, was beautiful enough to pierce the soul.

And as I stood there, transfixed, the dance began.

Out from the watching host, right around the circle, the dancers leaped. Men and women, and children too among them, with garlands of meadow flowers wound around their heads, they stepped forward down on to the shining floor, linked hands with their nearest neighbors and began to dance. First it was a stately progress with every move and gesture elegantly timed. Each spun their partner, stepped back, turned to the next dancer, bowed low or curtsied and resumed the dance with them. Anticlockwise around the rim they went, weaving complex loops and bows with every turn and spin. The watching crowd clapped and cheered and the music rose to a new crescendo with a sweet and melancholy joy.

It was all so beautiful, it took me a moment to remember myself and why I was there. Then I was running down the slope, along the curving path, until I came to the trellis arch and the fringes of the crowd. But the cheering throng had kept the six steps clear for me and I passed down them step by step to the very lip of the dance floor. Here the music was louder, sweeter than ever, and a perfume drifting from the vines above my head bathed me in a delicious embrace. I stood on the last step and shielding my eyes against the central light, looked out across the great expanse.

Max, Max, are you there?

Men, women, children, faces radiant with the joy of the dance, spinning past me, in and out, hair flying, skirts billowing, jackets lifting upward, mouths laughing, hands being held then dropped, grips being exchanged.

Max, I'm here.

A sea of whirling faces, eyes blank to everything but the music, racing toward me, past and away. All were beautiful, but it seemed to me that two types were on display. Some—long-haired and golden—were the people of the forest and the fair, tall, elegant, and radiant. Others were shorter and darker, more like the people of that other place, from which I had come, but which had long since faded from my mind. They were less beautiful than the people of the fair, but were still infused with the glory of the dance. Their eyes were wide, their mouths smiled. I looked, looked. . . .

Max . . .

Then, some way off, several couples distant, I caught sight of a face. It was for an instant only, blocked quickly by the head and hair of a laughing girl. But I needed only that single instant to *know*.

I cried out and craned my head, but the musicians raised the tempo, the dancers looped in upon themselves and a new set of couples spun themselves forward. He was swept away from me again, somewhere out of view.

My heart hammered in my chest. All around the edge of the dance floor the crowd had fallen silent now, watching the spectacle unfold. I stood on the step, under the vines, waiting for the dancers' patterns to weave Max back to me.

He was there. I'd almost caught him. Max was almost within my grasp.

viii

It isn't easy running full pelt over grass at night. I found that out soon enough. By the time I got to the fence at the edge of the park, I'd fallen over twice. The second time I fell I gashed my hand on a stone when I went over. But I got to the fence somehow, climbed it, and set off up the steep slope, across the bumpy, bouldery ground that marks the fringes of the reclaimed land.

This was worse than the park grass by a long way. There were lots of sharp rocks sticking out, and some of the earth was pretty loose. It took a lot of scrambling and a bit of swearing before I broke out on to the asphalt road that winds up the side of the hill to the old quarry site.

I'd been up here a couple of times on my bike. It was good to cycle down. But I'd never been beyond the fencing at the top. Only Max and Charlie had done that.

My body wanted me to stop. I was really out of shape. But I knew I couldn't stop, not now.

I stumbled off along the road, following the hill.

ix

The scent of the vine drowsed down through the music-charmed air and infected me with a quickening delight. I had him now: I was so close, I would be able to reach out and touch him. Any instant now. There he was again! Further off this time, but longer in my view. The joy of it! My eyes fell hungrily upon him. How did he look? His hair was longer than before—two months' longer. It fell and rose about his beautiful pale face as he danced with a golden-haired young man. His face was clear and radiant, almost impassive, but with the hint of a smile notched into the corners of his mouth. The light of the lanterns fell fully upon him. He was very handsome.

Then he swapped partners, the young man giving way to

a woman with brilliant red hair. Max took her hand, spun her around, and then the dance rotated and he was lost to me again.

Beside myself with agitation I stood on the stone lip, feeling my heart swell so full that I thought it might break. How soon would the dance end? When could I walk the final few steps to join with him at last? Could I yet catch his eye?

Then, without warning, a great weight fell upon me from within. I was a fool. The music and dancing had turned my head and I had forgotten the key thing.

Max had joined the dance. It was too late. He was lost to me. The beauty and grace of the dancers had overwhelmed me, but I knew—I could see with my own eyes—that Max was now at one with them. He would not remember me.

Suddenly I felt very small and tired and quite alone.

There was a movement in the crowd to my right, and a man pushed apart the hanging vines and stepped toward me. He wore a circlet of peonies in his hair.

"You are not too late, Charlie," Kit said. "All you need to do is step forward, and you will join him."

x

Up the hill, along the road, weary now, very weary.

And I came to the brow of the hill and the lorries' old turning circle. And there were the two padlocked wire gates, beside the bleached DANGER signs.

The lock was still in place, but one of the metal frames hung gaping and empty.

xi

"But he is in the dance," I said. "I could not get here before it started. I tried . . ." My voice trailed off, I wanted to cry.

"That's all right. You've done very well. You only just failed. But listen, you're not too late—even now—to catch him. He has not forgotten you yet, not quite, though the dance is working its magic upon him. Look out there—"

I looked: the dancing seemed to have reached a new level of speed and intensity. Each partner whirled and spun so fast that my eyes hurt to watch them. Max was nowhere to be seen.

"He is in the music's power," Kit said. "It weaves its way among his memories, disentangles them, combs them out, and lastly unwinds them behind him as he goes. When the dance is over he will be lost to you." Spoken so bluntly, this dug into my ribs as if it were a knife. I clenched my hair hard with agonized fingers.

"But you have one last chance," he went on. "You can join the dance too. Soon the tune will slow, the pattern will change and Max will be drawn near you, right here where you stand. Wait your moment well, then simply step in to join him."

"I do not know how to dance," I said.

"No need to. Everything here is given freely, you will fall into it easily enough. Here—" He raised his hands and carefully took the circlet of flowers from his head. This he placed gently on mine, smoothing down my hair so that it sat easily on top. I could feel the stalks prickling my brow.

"You need that," Kit said. "Everyone who dances here must wear one."

"I don't know . . . Will you dance?"

"No. My dance was long ago. Now watch and wait for your chance."

So we stood together on the stone lip, watching and waiting.

xii

I was still a long way off when I saw her. I had followed the road past the concrete huts with their boarded-up doors, round a bend and down toward the workings. The moonlight spilled down upon the exposed hillsides and illuminated the edges of the great black hole of the quarry pit cradled between them. It was a gaping emptiness. Moonlight didn't enter it. You could see nothing inside.

My sister was silhouetted in silver at the very edge of the hole, standing bolt upright, looking out across the void.

I knew exactly what she planned to do.

From where I was, up on the curve of the road, I called to her, but my voice was dry. I had no spit. Her name came out in a tattered croak.

I ran as fast as I could down the uneven road and I never took my eyes off her. Her figure jerked and juddered in my gaze as I careered down the slope.

Fifty meters away, as I opened my mouth to call to her again, my foot hit a rock in the middle of the road and I was falling. My foot was caught under the rock, my ankle twisted as I fell. I struck the ground, smashing my left arm hard against the road.

I probably screamed. I know when I raised my head, my face was covered in blood and dirt.

Spasms of pain throbbed in my ankle. It felt like it was going to burst with every pulse. I tried to raise myself, but a different pain lanced through my arm. My ankle dragged in the dust. Craning my head above the ground, I gasped out my sister's name.

Fifty meters away on the edge of the quarry, she was looking into emptiness.

xiii

"Isn't it beautiful?" Kit said. His arm rested on my shoulder.

Now the music slowed, as Kit had said it would, and the frenzied stepping of the dancers became smoother, more exaggerated, with arms out-flung and heads thrown back as if expressing a great sorrow. Their movements exerted an almost hypnotic effect. I could not take my eyes off them. By small degrees they rotated their positions and I readied myself for the first sign of Max. A drum sounded under the plaintive pipes and strings. I felt as if my heart beat only in reply.

Then, somewhere amid the music, I heard my name called. My heart leaped with joy, I craned my neck forward—and then at last, three or four couples distant, I saw him, Max, with his head swinging to and fro and his eyes serenely closed. I did not look to see who his partner was now—I had eyes only for him, sensing the great rotation of the dance as it drew my friend toward me.

The dance swung round one notch, and Max was now only three couples away. The music rose and fell. I could see the lights reflecting off the sweat in his hair. He tossed his head back and forth in time to the rhythm, his eyes quite closed. How peaceful he was, his sweet face unlined, expressionless. To me he was the still heart of this endless whirring spectacle of energy and light.

My name was called again. It came to me only faintly, almost submerged beneath the music. How could he sense me as he danced eyes shut? I was about to call in answer, when Kit squeezed my shoulder gently.

"Concentrate," he said. "You must wait your chance."

The music completed another repetition. Once more the dancers shifted round. Max was two couples from me now, so close I could see the embroidered collar on the silken jacket he was wearing. The ring of white flowers on his head seemed to sparkle as he moved. Tears studded my cheeks.

I readied myself to step forward. I was right on the lip of the dance floor, which was polished almost to a mirror by hundreds of quicksilver feet.

There was my name again. There was something

discordant about it—it jarred against the music. Max's lips didn't move. He was holding the hand of a dark-haired woman, his face expressionless, serene.

Kit spoke close against my ear. "Remember the fruit? You lost him then because you were distracted. You mustn't let that happen now."

The music switched, the dancers moved on. He was one couple distant, smiling now, his feet measuring elegant patterns as they drifted across the floor.

He spun the dark-haired woman around. I caught a flash of her pale face, her green eyes.

A flash of memory. A dull pain throbbed in my calf. I frowned.

They spun together, coming closer.

How pale he was, how strange his smile. He did not look at me, nor open his eyes. So how did he know to call my name, now for the fourth time? Why did it sound so harsh, so strident against the lilting music?

"Max." I whispered it, under my breath.

"Get ready." Kit's fingertips pressed into the nape of my neck.

Now the music shifted for the final time. The couple in front of me spun apart and moved away. And here was Max, dancing into the gap, his head held high.

The woman loosed his hand and danced back toward the center of the floor. But Max came toward me.

As he came, he did not look up but kept his eyes downcast toward his feet.

I stood ready, on the last step.

Everything slowed. I felt myself swallowed by the music; it rose up on all sides, engulfing me like a cocoon.

I looked at him. He was taller than I remembered, thinner too. His white shirt sparkled, his polished shoes and wet hair glistened in the dance light. His face and hands were ivory smooth and white.

So beautiful; and so unlike the Max I knew—

—except for his paleness. I'd seen him look like that somewhere before.

Now, almost close enough to touch, he raised his hand. It was pale as faded paper. Another memory. Something shambling among dark trees. Still Max did not look at me.

I lifted my own hand up, stretched it out.

"Go join him, Charlie," Kit said. "Now."

The waiting hand was palm out, ready to help me down.

"Dance with him, Charlie," Kit said. "This is what you desire."

I began to move forward. Then Max raised his head and his eyes met mine.

And I saw them, the living eyes I never thought I'd see again, and a thrill of victory stabbed me through. But the living eyes I saw were joyless, they looked on me with a sorrow that turned to ashes the smile their own face wore. And I seemed to look right past them too, see them also white and sightless, drifting in the murk.

"Take his hand and leap!" Kit shouted.

I reached out.

Max's hand swung upward.

Our hands clasped.

I did not leap. I pulled him up.

And found he had no weight at all. I lost my balance, toppled backward, and as I did so, heard Kit's furious shouting, "Dance, you fool! Dance!"

Behind it, a voice that was not Kit's sounded out loud and shrill.

And the music exploded into a discordant scream.

I fell back, holding Max's hand. All across the dance floor, the dancers froze rigid where they stood, arms out, hair flung back, heads distended, leering. Their beauty fell from them, slid from their features as their graceful bodies thinned and shriveled to bone and gristle beneath their clothes.

A cry of fury rose up all around and loudest of all was the scream of rage from where Kit stood. His high-pitched snarling echoed in my ears as if he were crouching by me as I fell, but I did not see his face.

I fell. And Max fell too, toward me but away from me at the same time, free of my hand now, free of the dance. And I saw that he was once again wearing his old T-shirt and jeans and the Nike trainers with the imprint on the soles. The sweat in his hair had turned to water and his clothes were soaked right through. The flowers in his hair were river-weed. His eyes no longer looked at me. They were passionless, serene. Then, as I watched, he drew apart and vanished from my sight.

The music and the screaming and the shouting rose to a high crescendo. I fell away from it all with a sudden speed, and the lights of the dance went out.

Thirty-Two

As my sister dropped, I raised a shout that echoed off the hills.

She fell to the ground on the lip of the quarry, head flung back toward me, one foot hanging out over the edge. She didn't move. The moonlight and the night chill spilled over her and over me. I was shivering uncontrollably.

It took a few minutes to crawl the remaining distance balanced on one leg, one arm. My knee scuffled in the dirt. The cold numbed the pain in my arm.

I hauled myself into a sitting position beside her. Charlie lay on her back, face looking up at the stars. Her breathing was heavy, like one in deep sleep. I brushed her fringe back from her forehead, sweeping away a few tattered grasses that had found their way into her hair.

One of her arms was outstretched on the ground. I lifted her hand and held it in mine. Then I sat there, stroking her forehead and talking to her softly. Above us the cold moon shone down. It was high between the hills and its light flooded into the black hole of the quarry pit, filling the emptiness.

And after a little time, my sister opened her eyes and smiled at me, and spoke my name.

Don't miss the
spellbinding fantasy thriller
by Jonathan Stroud

Buried
Fire